SATURN NIGHT FEVER

SATURN NIGHT FEVER

SYLVIA STRYKER SPACE CASE MYSTERY #3

LINESVILLE PUBLIC LIBRARY
111 PENN ST
PO BOX 97
LINESVILLE, PA 16424
☎ 814-683-4354

DIANE VALLERE

Copyright Page
SATURN NIGHT FEVER
Sylvia Stryker Space Case #3
A Polyester Press Publication

All rights reserved. No part of this book may be used or reproduced by any means, graphic, electronic, or mechanical, including photocopying, recording, taping or by any information storage retrieval system without the written permission of the publisher except in the case of brief quotations embodied in critical articles and reviews.

This is a work of fiction. Characters, places, and events are the product of the author's imagination or are used fictitiously. Any resemblance to real people, companies, institutions, organizations, or incidents is entirely coincidental.

Library of Congress Control Number: 2018958291

Trade paperback edition
Copyright © 2018 Diane Vallere
ISBN: 9781939197528

DEDICATION

To my parents, Mary and Don Vallere, who respected the writing process enough for me to write this book while keeping me firmly on earth with pizza and pretzels.

MOON UNIT CREW AND PASSENGER MANIFEST

AstroNovas: aerial military squadron.

Cat: Sylvia's robot built to resemble a cat. Acts as an alarm clock, computer, flashlight, and more.

Champion, Zeke: Son of spaceship repairman. Expert on hacking and space drone technology. Friend of Sylvia Stryker.

Champion, Hubble: Spaceship repairman. Zeke's dad.

Dusk, Mattix: Space courier. Taught Sylvia Hapkido fighting style in exchange for repairs and modifications to space pod.

Doc Edison: Head of Medi-Bay. Cranky. Low tolerance for secret missions. Drinks whiskey.

Faarstar, Omicron: Baddest space pirate renegade of a new generation of evil, Inheritor to Cheung Qidd's space pirate network. New threat to the galaxy. Dangerous and dirty. A little stinky too.

Gremlons: alien race that lives on Colony 7. Pink. Lack the ability to defend themselves. Usually work in the entertainment industry. Have fifty teeth and are cagey. Shrink when scared.

Grey Aliens: interchangeable and indiscernible aliens who work as space pirate henchmen. Often tattooed with markings to indicate ownership and a way to tell them apart.

Grey One: The first grey alien to appear in the book. Has a "1" tattooed on his hand.

Grey Two: The second grey alien to appear in the book. Has a "2" tattooed on his hand.

Grey Three: The third grey alien to appear in the book. Has a "3" tattooed on his hand.

Grey Four: I know you're smart, so I'll let you figure this one out on your own.

Ivi: Female Martian. Communications lieutenant aboard Moon Unit Mini 7.2. Small, green. Wears false eyelashes but is otherwise hairless.

Kentaro: Medic. Injured in war between Mars and Venus. Walks with a limp. Owns T-Fal, his personal robot.

Marshall, Vaan: Youngest member of Federation Council. Sylvia's first love. Recused himself from the vote to convict Jack Stryker for collusion with pirates. From Plunia, the same planet as Sylvia.

Neptune: Head of security on Moon Unit Corporation. Tough guy. Big muscles. Believes in word efficiency. Thinks nobody knows his secrets. Is wrong.

Pika: pink Gremlon alien. Troublemaker. Friend of Sylvia. Kidnap victim.

Qidd, Cheung: Evil space pirate. Serving life sentence on Colony 13. Terminal.

Rune, Rebel: Engineer aboard Moon Unit Mini 7 series. Highly recommended, last minute hire.

Stryker, Jack: Sylvia's dad. Has been serving time in a Federation Council prison. Recent intel suggests he is not guilty of the crimes he's been accused of. At this point his guilt and or innocence are unconfirmed.

Stryker, Sylvia: Space Academy dropout. Half Plunian and half Human. Smart. Has photographic memory, lavender skin, and excellent problem-solving abilities. Grew up on dry ice farm. Hates space pirates. Has tiny problem blindly following orders and does not like Martians!

T-Fal: robot belonging to Kentaro. Assembled from

recycled non-stick aluminum cookware, including pressure cooker head and rice cooker torso. All settings have been reprogrammed for tasks more robot-like than cooking rice (though one setting had remained, since robot's owner enjoys steamed rice as a snack.)

Williams, Hale: African American physician who performed the first prototype open-heart surgery.

Yoka: pink Gremlon boy. Short and plump. Spokesperson for Gremlons on board ship. Possible troublemaker.

1: IMPACT

When Neptune said I fought like a girl, I did the only respectable thing. I hit him. That's not to say it's a good idea for dropouts from the space academy to strike their newly-appointed superiors, but in this case, he deserved it.

In the two versions of the story that will be told of the incident, at least one will contain the fact that technically, I was in training. Technically, the only reason we were on the helipad on the corner of Neptune's property was because the helipad was a convenient place to practice. Technically, I was being paid a small sponsorship fee to test the durability of new uniforms designed for Moon Unit Corporation, and technically, the only way I could fully know if the uniforms were durable were to see how they held up when I threw a punch.

Neptune's version might include slight variations.

"In case you haven't noticed, I *am* a girl," I said.

Neptune was bigger, older, and more experienced than I was, and he probably had more important things to do than spend the day teaching me defensive maneuvers. But never graduating had left me with relatively few channels to advance my learning.

After Moon Unit 6 returned from Venus, Neptune contacted me via the comm device implanted in my ear and offered me free room and board in exchange for lessons to pick up where my interrupted education had left off. I'd dropped out when my dad was arrested so I could help my mom with the family dry ice mines. Neptune's offer to teach me gave us both something of value. I'd accepted, more for me than for him. I'm selfish that way.

"You know why you were almost incapacitated on our last moon trek?" he asked. "Because you dropped your guard. You thought size and skill were enough to beat your enemy. You fought fair. You fought like a woman."

"Oh, so now I'm a woman?" I countered. "I grew up fast."

It wasn't that Neptune treated me like a girl or a woman. He treated me like a student. And most of the time I was okay with that. But the voice in my head that I didn't want to listen to wondered why someone like Neptune spent time training someone like me. It was a voice that hadn't had much to question since my dad was arrested.

Any attention paid to me usually had strings

attached. Retribution for my dad's crimes, or the novelty of my half Plunian background in a world where lavender women were now rare. More than once I'd fended off advances when I saw where they were headed. I developed a thick skin and narrowed my social circle to a very tight group.

But despite the fact that Neptune was a muscular wall of taciturn authority, or maybe because of it, I was attracted to him. I doubted it was the black military-issue cargo gear he wore (did he buy his clothes in bulk?) or the intimidating stance he'd perfected long before I met him (arms crossed, feet shoulder-width apart). I'd never been attracted to men in power—in fact, power was a pretty tried-and-true turn-*off*. I didn't know what it was about Neptune that made my lavender skin glow at the least opportune times. I only knew it was important to me to prove to him that I was different. Today, different meant throwing a non-girly punch.

He grabbed my wrist and closed my fingers into a fist. His hand was twice the size of mine—tawny against my lavender coloring. "You have to toughen up, Stryker. You're smart, and you learn information fast, but instincts don't come from a book."

"I learned how to fight by an accredited Hapkido master. Or have you already forgotten that I dropped you with a sweeping kick because you underestimated me?"

He let go of my fist and pointed at me. "Don't let that go to your head. Success is built on failure. If you learn anything from these lessons, learn that. Failure is your friend."

"I thought failure wasn't an option? The flight director of Earth's space shuttle program said it, right? His biography was required reading."

"You didn't read the book. That's a made-up quote from a movie script. The flight director liked the line so much he used it for the title of his biography. Lesson number two: check your source. I thought you knew that by now."

I didn't tell Neptune that I hadn't read the book because the course took place after I dropped out. I'm pretty sure lesson number three is to keep your weaknesses to yourself.

"Repeat it back to me."

"Blah, blah, check your source."

"Repeat what I told you about failure."

"'Failure is my friend.'"

"Remember that." He turned around and walked a few feet away from me and then turned back. "If you think you can fight because you dropped me—once—then you'll get complacent. Don't forget what happened the last time you got complacent."

How could I forget? I almost died. It didn't help that the fight had been four against one or that my oxygen supply had been cut off, rendering me helpless. My opponents knew my weakness and used it against me. Nothing fair about it. I didn't want to admit it, but

Neptune was right. I'd falsely assumed I could defend myself without too much effort, and my false sense of confidence had worked against me.

"Go again," he said. He bent his knees slightly and prepared for my attack. I swung my arms forward and backward, giant half circles to limber up my shoulders, and felt a seam tear. "Hold on. Uniform malfunction. Moon Unit Corporation thinks they can cut corners by using a different supplier, but the last six uniforms I tested fell apart."

"Where?"

"Shoulder."

"Turn around."

I turned and pointed to where I'd felt the split. "What am I supposed to tell them this time? 'Looks good but you can't throw a girly punch'?"

I felt Neptune tug the split fabric together. Even though I wasn't looking at him, just the graze of his fingertips against my shoulder blade made me flush.

"Why are you wasting your time with uniforms?"

"Someday the name 'Sylvia Stryker' will be synonymous with space uniforms. After our trip to Venus, the publicity company who planned the hype around the Moon Units contacted me to wear test their prototypes. It's a little cash on the side between treks and all things considered, I can use the money. I can't crash here forever."

I knew Neptune wouldn't pursue the conversation.

He understood my predicament: no planet, no family, no home. He was with me the night space pirates destroyed everything I'd ever known. The only reason I agreed to train with him was because there's a certain security in spending time with someone who prioritized silence over small talk. I could learn a lot from Neptune and I knew it.

He could learn from me too. I wasn't sure he knew that. Yet.

Neptune's loner lifestyle suited him, but I was glad that he begrudgingly allowed me to coexist on his property. Not one to mooch, I made sure to bring what I could to the table. Enter Mattix Dusk, space courier (and my Hapkido instructor) who traveled between the thirteen colonies under Federation Control, to pick up and deliver anything that needed to be picked up or delivered. I introduced the two men and they worked out a mutually acceptable deal. Mattix had use of the helipad and a place to crash while on the Kuiper Belt. Neptune had access to Mattix's courier contacts and suppliers. And for the foreseeable future, I had not one but two mentors who could further my education.

Where Neptune was tall, tawny, and solid muscle, Mattix looked like a piece of worn leather in loose-fitting castoff clothes. Tanned skin, bleached hair worn in a ponytail, and ragamuffin clothes suited him. His job as courier put him in front of shady characters, and he passed along his two most important pieces of advice: look like you have less than the other guy and learn to take care of yourself.

Whatever direction my lesson was supposed to go was interrupted by a swiftly approaching space pod. I looked at the sky and watched it glide toward us. It was the Dusk Driver, the space pod that belonged to Mattix.

I smiled and waved while backing up so he could land. As his space pod drew closer, alarm bells rang out from the nearby towers. His speed was too fast. He was going to crash. And if I didn't get out of the way, I'd burn up in the wreckage.

Neptune reached the same conclusion before I did. How do I know? When I tore my attention from the incoming space pod to tell Neptune something was wrong, I saw him charge toward me. The impact knocked me to the ground.

Either Neptune knew what was happening and wanted to save me, or he was trying to make a point.

From the bank of dirt alongside the helipad, the space pod jerked to a halt and then hovered two feet above the ground. Mattix knew better than to approach at the speed he had, but he'd compensated for the potential accident by activating the ship's invisible buffer: a two foot "bumper" of static electricity that kept the exterior from contacting another surface. It operated much the same way as two magnets held in close proximity. The dueling forcefields pushed away from each other, making it impossible to touch. Mattix wouldn't have activated the buffer shield unless something was wrong.

I scrambled to my feet and, keeping my center of gravity low, approached the space pod. Mattix wouldn't allow anyone else to navigate the ship without reason, which made what I saw even scarier.

The ship was being flown on autopilot.

2: TRAINING MISSION

I pulled my goggles down to protect my eyes from the clouds of dust swirling around and tried to look inside. The buffer kept me from getting too close. But I didn't have to be up close and personal to see that the interior of the space pod was empty.

There were a few reasons a space pod would be flown without a pilot. Return to home base had been activated. Someone else had programmed it for diversion. Or something had happened to the driver.

There was only one option I liked, and even that came with a slew of questions.

"What do you see?"

"The pod is empty. Dashboard panel lights are blinking white."

"Random or in a pattern?"

I squinted through my goggles and waved my hand in front of them to clear away the dust. "Pattern. It's a message."

"Decipher."

Neptune was using this as a teachable moment. I turned toward him and rolled my eyes, though between the space goggles and the dust, I wasn't sure he could see them.

"Quit rolling your eyes and decipher the message."

I stared back into the space pod. The pattern of lights blinked for several seconds and then repeated. After three sessions, I had it down. *The ship has been compromised. This is not a drill. Repeat, this is not a drill. Details in passenger.*

Neptune pulled me away from the pod and stepped up to the window. The invisible buffer pushed his legs backward, but his strong thighs countered the resistance. Where I hadn't been able to get any closer than a foot away, Neptune was right up against the fiberglass exterior.

"Dismantle the drive," he said over his shoulder.

He took this teachable moment thing seriously. I went behind the ship and squatted down by the exterior reactor. Mattix's pod ran on dilithium crystal rods which were inserted at the back of the vehicle under a hinged panel. The small size of the ship made it lightweight and fast, but it couldn't travel long distances without the potent fuel source. I used a retractor to unscrew the panel and remove the rod. As soon as it was out of the fuel chamber, the buffer turned off, and the pod fell to the ground. A larger puff of moon dust exploded by my gravity boots and then filled the air. I slipped the mouthpiece to my oxygen tube between my lips and inhaled.

Neptune, either unprepared or mistakenly believing he was invincible, coughed. He jogged a few feet from where the pod landed and leaned over, inhaling less cloudy air.

One of the main rules of a security team: don't leave a team member behind.

I pulled a splitter out from a pocket, fitted it onto my small oxygen tank, and joined Neptune. I held out the mouthpiece and kept my thumb on the button that would split the release of clean air between us. He put the mouthpiece between his lips and I pressed the button. Ha! My own teachable moment! I stood a little straighter and grinned (as much as I could with breathing apparatus in my mouth).

After a few hits of oxygen, Neptune removed his mouthpiece. "You didn't act according to protocol," he said.

"Oh, come on! You're catching me up on the lessons I missed when I dropped out of the academy, right? I already know when there's a threat it's better to have all team members operating at full capacity than to let one go down while the other takes point. You couldn't breathe so I sacrificed a moment of staring into an empty space pod to give you some of my oxygen. It was the right thing. Now you're all better and you can go back to lecturing me. We haven't missed a beat."

"What if there were hitchhikers on the space pod? What if a stowaway was hoping for an opportunity just like that to deboard and get away? What if the ship was wired with an explosive device triggered by the removal of the crystals? What if there's an emergency on board and you lost valuable time giving me oxygen I didn't need?"

"You ran away from the pod to get clean air. You needed the oxygen."

"I ran away from the pod so I could run diagnostics from a distance."

"You couldn't breathe. Between the space pod and you, I chose to help you. The pod isn't going anywhere without the crystals. Besides, I already know this was a training mission. You probably had Mattix send his pod back on autopilot to test me. And I did everything by the book—except for giving you oxygen, and I deserve extra credit for that because we haven't covered those lessons yet."

"Stryker."

"What? You know I'm right. Admit it. 'This is not a drill'? You could have come up with something a little better than that. The suggestion that it was a drill is right there in the message. That tells me you have the ability to program Mattix's space pod. And we just happen to be training next to the coordinates where it landed. Too much coincidence."

Neptune towered over me and stared down. He put his hands on my shoulders, holding me in place. He was at least a head taller than me and probably weighed twice as much and even though I knew he was my ally, I also recognized for a moment how he'd gotten his reputation in the galaxy. The dude was intense.

"This was a mission designed to let you practice disabling a ship. Mattix Dusk agreed to send his space pod back here on one condition. It had to do with the message that was programmed into the dashboard."

"You would think if I knew it was a training mission after decoding the message, I wouldn't have taken it seriously. I'm surprised you even conceded that point. Mr. There-are-threats-everywhere."

"Stand still," Neptune said. He wrapped his muscular arm around me and pulled me into his chest. The contact knocked the wind out of me. With his other hand, he unsheathed his space gun and fired. My face was pressed into his black space militia shirt, and I cursed the fact that half of my oxygen was now running to his mouthpiece because I couldn't breathe. I pounded my fist on his chest and wriggled away. "Point taken! Now, let me go!"

He relaxed his arm, and I spun out from his embrace. I turned toward the space pod to see the damage he'd have to explain to Mattix.

Either Neptune and Mattix went all out in designing a training mission, or Mattix was in trouble. Because lying face down on the dirt halfway between the space pod and us was the body of a dead grey alien. And in his outstretched hand, tattooed with a "1," was a ray gun that would have vaporized both me and my teacher if given the chance.

3: THE PASSENGER

I recognized the marking on the grey's hand. It indicated ownership by Omicron Faarstar, the space pirate who had taken over the territories once controlled by the now-incarcerated and terminally ill Cheung Qidd. And Cheung Qidd, in his days of better health, was the space pirate who my dad was accused of colluding with. The literal meaning of Omicron Faarstar was "Star Far Star," which was a pretty silly name for a space pirate if you asked me. If I ever met him face to face, I wasn't sure if I'd share that thought.

"The number on his hand—that's a pirate marking," I said.

"Yes," Neptune said.

I shivered. "Is he dead?"

"Yes."

"Was he going to vaporize us?"

"Yes."

I nudged the alien's hand with the toe of my gravity boot. The hand dissolved into the ground, leaving the vaporizer behind. Watching the alien turn to dust with that little contact made me wonder about the cloud of dust that had swirled around my and Neptune's legs moments before. I'd always thought of it as moon dust, but it seemed just as likely to be disintegrated aliens. Gotta be honest—that creeped me out a little.

"Report," Neptune said.

"You just kicked some alien butt. I think the lesson plan is over."

"Stryker. Focus. What is your assessment? What is your containment strategy?"

I stood in the Neptune stance, not to mock him but because I'd learned it provided the greatest level of stability and balance when faced with an unknown danger. "Threat level unknown. Presence of one alien confirmed."

Grey aliens were like roaches. Where there was one, there were usually more. They lacked individuality and were virtually impossible to tell apart.

Neptune nodded. "Strategy?"

"Grey One terminated so known threat has been eliminated," I continued. "Coded message on dash panel suggests there is intel inside. Suggested containment strategy: bag samples from Grey One. Move space pod to isolation for full equipment inspection. Action plan: find passenger and plan possible mission based on information contained within."

Neptune nodded. Once. He switched his space gun to the vacuum setting and held it toward the grey alien's body. As I watched, the ashy residue of Grey One turned into dust that was sucked up into the chamber of his gun. When Neptune finished, he switched the vacuum setting off and twisted the ring around the gun to lock the contents into a storage chamber until he could have it analyzed in a lab.

The second parts of my plan—moving the space pod to an isolated point to examine it—would be more difficult. I didn't doubt Neptune could fly a space pod. I'd watched Mattix do it enough times that even I could navigate in a pinch. But the crystals had been removed, and once they contacted the atmosphere, there was no telling if they'd been corrupted. Reinserting them could introduce an unknown deterioration element into the fuel chamber.

"Suggest identifying the message before moving the pod," I said.

Neptune nodded again. I assumed he'd already thought of that but had kept it to himself to see if I'd catch up.

Maybe there was something to this whole blacklisted-from-the-space-academy/private-tutor thing after all.

I approached the pod. I wore black gloves made from a durable and flexible fabric that should have been used on the uniform. I wiped the convex fiberglass bubble and looked inside for signs of "the passenger" the coded message in the dashboard had alluded to, slowly fearing a whole different possibility.

I turned around. "The code said there were details in the passenger. What if the alien was the passenger? Maybe that whole message was a trap? If Grey One hadn't aimed a vaporizer at us, we might have trusted him."

"Greys are bred to take orders. They execute tasks. They're the front lines of the space pirate armies. Grey One was marked by Faarstar. If a grey was on Mattix's pod, then it's safe to assume Faarstar has Mattix. Grey One was not the passenger."

The reality of that hit me. If the grey wasn't the passenger, then the passenger was still on board. And with no crystal in the fuel chamber, the air quality would have become unbreathable for anyone without oxygen. But activating the buffer zone would have required all oxygen to be off, because a malfunctioning buffer would lead to a crash, and a crash fueled by oxygen would create an explosion.

Those thoughts materialized in a moment, and instead of asking Neptune for advice or waiting to see what he wanted to do, I undid the release latches for the dome of the ship. When all sixteen latches were open, I pried the dome apart from the base of the pod and flipped it over itself onto the ground. Alien cooties swirled around from the impact. I waved my hand to clear the air and scanned the interior. In seconds, I identified the passenger. A small, white toy in the shape of a cat, wedged underneath the base of the navigator's seat.

It was my robot kitten. During nights on my home planet, after working in the dry ice mines with my mom, I'd rewired Cat's circuits so he functioned more in line with my needs. He served as my alarm clock, meowing at first sunlight; stored data that I encoded in digital files; and held files of history, instruction manuals, and the entire contents of a twentieth-century Encyclopedia Britannica that I'd bought from back channels.

He also recorded messages that could be replayed by digital projection.

I climbed into the pod and jiggled Cat until he was loose. Neptune was familiar with Cat and what he could do, but he didn't know why Cat was in Mattix Dusk's space pod. I did, and it had to do with a certain pink Gremlon girl who'd been living on Neptune's property with me. Pika.

I set Cat on the ground and activated his projection capabilities. A cone of light came out from his eyes like a flashlight. I set him on the ground and aimed him at the rear panel of the space pod. The image was a pink Gremlon girl, just like I'd suspected.

"Now you be a good cat, okay? Go get Sylvia and tell her we need her help. But don't tell the giant." The projection of her eyes got wide. "If he finds out I went to Saturn, he'll be mad mad mad. I know Sylvia kept my secret. She promised." Pika reached out and patted Cat on the head, which was weird to watch since Cat was filming the message. As Pika's hand got closer, it appeared out of proportion and I leaned away instinctively. "Bye-bye, Cat," she said. And then she picked him up and the message went black.

4: GRAND THEFT SPACESHIP

I'd first met Pika on a moon trek to Ganymede, Jupiter's largest moon. It was the same trek where I'd met Neptune, and it had taken a lot less time to trust her than him. Gremlons were friendly, funny, and non-threatening by nature. They could grow or shrink at will, usually worked in the entertainment sector, and lacked the instincts to defend themselves. It was this last reason that had led Neptune to become Pika's unofficial caretaker, letting her live on his property in the far reaches of the galaxy. Neptune was one of the most feared men in the universe, but between jobs, he looked out for a defenseless alien girl who called him a giant. I didn't think a lot of people got to see that side of him.

Pika's exposure to Neptune had been good for her. She may never know how to fight, but she had a talent for finding things—especially small, shiny ones. It had been my assessment that she needed a strong female role model in her life too. Seeing no other candidates for the job, I assigned it to myself, and when Mattix asked if I wanted to join him on a trip to Saturn to trade raw graphite for unfiltered moon dust, I suggested Pika go in my place. She'd hopped back and forth between her feet and then asked me to make her a special courier uniform. I didn't have the heart to tell her there was no such thing, so I crafted one out of a bolt of silver fabric Mattix had brought back from his last trip to Uranus. She wore the uniform the entire week before they left.

"Pika went to Saturn with Mattix?" Neptune asked.

"It does sound that way."

"You knew."

"We may have discussed it."

"You let an ill-equipped Gremlon travel with an independent space courier to a planet under pirate control?"

I put my hands on my hips. "Pika was not ill-equipped. I let her take Cat. You may have erased his databanks from the trip to Venus, but I added a whole lot of upgrades after I took him apart."

Neptune glared at me. This time, I glared back. We'd never talked about that—about how I'd stolen files about Neptune from a border patrol agent and how the day after I agreed to live on Neptune's property, the files suddenly vanished from Cat's internal file storage.

I'd never acknowledged what he did. I also never told him he was too late—I'd read the files the night before.

The information—that Neptune operated as a bounty hunter before taking a job with Moon Unit Corporation—was simply one more fact to the mental file I was collecting on him. It meant his skills went beyond military training and his loyalties weren't solely with Federation Council. Considering I wasn't a fan of theirs myself, the info on Neptune was a positive.

"Pika isn't like you and me," he said.

"And that's a bad thing?" I looked away, and my eyes rested on Cat. Neptune's secrets weren't the issue anymore. "I trusted Mattix. And while what you said may be all or only partly true, our priorities are to find Pika and bring her back. You can lecture me when we're done. Don't waste time turning this into a teachable moment."

No matter how wrong it might have been to let Pika get on board that space pod with Mattix, now wasn't the time to talk about it. "All we know from that message is that Pika is on Saturn. Considering she can't fly a space pod and this space pod belongs to Mattix, I think it's safe to assume he's on Saturn with her so it's not like she's out there all by herself."

Neptune moved to the back of the pod and opened the cargo hatch. "You're wrong," he said.

I joined him and saw the one thing worse than Pika's cry for help. The body of my favorite space courier, dressed in mismatched castoffs, looking pale beneath his leathery skin. Bleached hair, normally secured at the back of his head, moved in the breeze. Whatever judgment I'd shown in letting Pika go with Mattix was blown to bits.

My breath caught in my throat and I instinctively stepped closer to the space pod. Neptune put out his arm to block my approach. "We don't know what happened here," he said.

"Mattix is my friend," I said, swallowing a lump. "He needs help." I pushed Neptune's arm away and pressed my fingers against the side of Mattix's throat. There was no pulse.

"He's dead," Neptune said.

"Mattix was one of the only friends I have left. He can't be dead. He was on a routine mission. If he's dead, then Pika is—" The lump returned, and I looked away and blinked rapidly. I didn't want Neptune to see me cry.

"Then Pika is alone and needs our help. There's nothing you can do for Mattix anymore." Neptune's voice held a rare note of consolation. "I'll notify the authorities to collect his body. Get your gear together. We deploy for Saturn from the helipad in the morning."

"How are we going to get there? You said yourself the Dusk Driver has been compromised."

"We'll use the materializer."

"To where? You can't just make us show up on Saturn. We need a ship. We need equipment."

"We're going to hijack a Moon Unit."

In other words, I'd just been enrolled in an advanced level course.

***

I mourned Mattix's murder that night while MPs arrived and collected his body. Neptune advised me to keep my distance. For what he had planned, we needed a low profile. A hole inside me, left in place of the friendship I could no longer rely on, ached like an injury. The only way to ease the pain was to focus on finding Pika and bringing Mattix's killer to justice. It didn't matter that Neptune's plan involved illegal actions. I was in.

Moon Unit Corporation owned a fleet of spaceships designed for paid passenger travel to various tourist destinations throughout the galaxy. The first time I "worked" for them, I'd hacked into the database and uploaded my files on top of those of an existing crew member. There are better ways to get a job.

The second time, I'd been there legitimately. And after what had happened on that trip, I knew they considered me not only an asset, but a part of the Moon Unit family. It was through the recommendation of the captain that I'd been given the job of wear-testing samples of the new uniforms, a job that paid me enough to establish a life between trips.

Any other Plunian would have used the money to buy a plot of land and start a farm—what Plunians were known for. When our planet was blown up, the major supplier of dry ice for the galaxy went with it. Federation Council had established a Plunian Relief Fund too, intended to colonize an underdeveloped planet for those who'd lost their homes and teaching new trades for families who'd been left with nothing.

There were two problems with that plan. One: thanks to rumors about my dad, my fellow Plunians saw me as the daughter of the man who'd brought destruction to their homes and didn't really want me around.

And two: I'd recently learned the rumors weren't true.

I'd joined Pika and Neptune on his property and agreed to look out for Pika in exchange for my lessons. When Mattix first invited me to join him on a trip, I suggested Pika instead. ("Helping out," I called it, though behind her back there were air quotes). He laughed at the idea. Pika knew relatively little about the galaxy but now that she'd been exposed to things like murder and violence, she needed a survival education too. The trip with Mattix would be good, I'd thought, since I knew he could defend her. And I let her take Cat as an extra safety precaution.

I hoisted my black backpack onto my shoulder and pulled a suitcase along behind me. Inside were six test uniforms, four canisters of oxygen, sleep gear, goggles, gloves, and gadgets. There were also a dozen packs of freeze-dried Plunian ice cream because I didn't expect a stolen spaceship to have much in the way of comfort food.

Neptune was waiting for me by the transport pad on the edge of his property. "Have you traveled by materializer before?"

"No."

"You'll be fine. Get on."

"That's it? 'Get on'? Aren't you going to tell me what to expect or where we're going to end up or—" I heard a sound, at first low and then increasing in volume. Neptune stepped away from the computer and joined me. I looked at my hands, glowing purple (my normal color) with a white outline (definitely not normal!). Neptune put his hand on mine and held it. The white outline glowed around his tawny hand too. My pulse picked up. He squeezed. I squeezed back. And then just as the sound reached deafening levels, the world as I knew it imploded, taking us with it.

5: REMATERIALIZATION

The blackness blew up into an explosion of colors. Every color I'd ever imagined and sixteen more that I hadn't. More mesmerizing than the sparkles that trailed a moving Venusian. More temporary than ice in a hot climate. The colors were there and then gone.

Which is when I realized with a letdown that we'd landed in Moon Unit's Security section—the most utilitarian part of a spaceship.

Once I realized I'd arrived with my gear (and my person) intact, I jumped up and down. "What a rush!" I said. "Is that how you travel? All the time? Do you love it? How'd you get a materializer on your property? Are they going to find us? Should we hide? Where should we hide? That was amazing!"

"Stryker."

"Oh, come on! You can't honestly say you're so jaded you don't know that was cool."

Neptune pulled out an infrared thermometer. It was made of hard gray plastic curved into a hook. He held the base and aimed the end at my temple. The device beeped twice. "You're hot. Sit."

"Of course I'm hot. I'm half Plunian and our temperature runs hotter"—a wave of vertigo hit me and I swayed—"whoa." I put my hand out for balance. The only thing within reach was Neptune's chest. It worked in terms of giving me something stable to hold onto, but not so much for cooling me off. My lavender skin glowed as it always did when I got excited. This time I was going to blame it on the experience of rematerializing.

"Sit."

"I'll just sit," I said as if it were my idea. I looked for a bench. There wasn't a bench. Where was the seating? There were seats in the last two Moon Units—why not this one? Oh, that's right, because it was part of a series of Mini Moon Units. This was Moon Unit Mini 7.2. I turned around and saw the only other seat available. Inside the holding cell.

"You know what? I'll stand."

"Sit."

"Fine. This is a new Moon Unit, so it's clean, right?" I lowered myself to the ground. The floor, coated in magnetic paint to interact with the soles of our gravity boots and help counter the effects of the ship's zero gravity when we were in flight, was cold against the back of my thighs. I had to remember that for my report on the sample uniforms. They needed to be able to provide a better barrier against external elements.

"Okay, so we're here. Now what? Do you know how to fly a Moon Unit? Don't you think they're going to notice when the ship leaves the docking station? Aren't you afraid of being arrested or losing your job? Have you thought this through?"

"We're on the ship. What would you do next?"

"This is the hardest course *ever*."

"Focus."

I didn't want to admit to Neptune that the rematerializer had left me slightly loopy. On our last trek, he'd instructed me to use the High Velocity Pressure Transport System to quickly get from one side of the ship to the other, and too much HVPTS had had negative side effects. It was because of my Plunian side. I didn't want anybody to think there were things I couldn't do because I was part Plunian. *Get it together, Sylvia.*

"You need a crew. You can't fly a Moon Unit yourself."

He nodded once.

"And you need a ship full of passengers otherwise the crew will get suspicious."

He nodded again.

"We need a cover story. How about this: I hack into the Moon Unit staff database and notify the second level crew that this is a training simulation. That'll explain why there aren't any passengers or operational restaurants on board the ship. We take off before anybody has a chance to figure out what we did. We tell the staff to sign confidentiality agreements and waive their right to discuss the trip."

"Keep going."

"Doc can run physicals at check-in—"

"We can't use Doc. He knows too much."

Doc Edison was the head doctor who'd been with Moon Unit Corporation since the beginning. He was cranky and had a low tolerance for security staff, especially those whose name started with "N" and ended with "eptune." My affiliation with said security staffer didn't seem to have much bearing on my relationship with Doc, who seemed to find me charming.

"What if something goes wrong? What if we find Pika and she's hurt? I'm not doing this and putting a hijacked ship full of duped second-string Moon Unit staff at risk. We need a doctor. We need a *real* doctor. Isn't it riskier to find someone we don't know than to use someone we do?"

"Hack the database and send a notice out to the second lieutenants of each station. They won't ask questions. Tell them to show up with current medical papers. We'll use the computer in Medi-Bay to diagnose any problems we have while we're in flight."

"I still say we need Doc," I said.

"Noted."

"We need directions to Saturn."

"The Moon Unit has GPS. I'll program the coordinates

and use warp drive and we'll be at Saturn in a day."

"And then what?"

"This is your mission, Stryker. You tell me."

I didn't believe for a second that Neptune would let me design a mission, but I wasn't going to tell him that. This was a chance I'd wanted my whole life and I knew I could do it. But the knowledge that it wasn't a school project or a training module but the real need to save Pika and catch Mattix's killer brought on a type of focus I hadn't felt before.

"You're going to have to be the face of the mission," I said. "I'm an unknown. And based on my family history, a lot of crew members still think I'm unreliable. You need to suit up in uniform and be the captain."

"Is that it?"

"No." I hesitated, because the next thing I was going to say were words I never thought I'd say again in my life. "We need another ally. Someone who has inside knowledge of Federation Council and space pirates and isn't afraid to break a couple of rules. Do you know anybody who fits that profile?"

Neptune nodded. "Yes, and so do you. Your father, Jack Stryker."

6: ONE BIG IF

"Do you think you can trust him?" Neptune asked.

"On our recent trip to Venus, you told me Jack Stryker wasn't guilty. I went to Captain Ryder to report you for spreading propaganda, and she confirmed your intel." I'd never told Neptune that I'd gone behind his back, but I'd been so mad at him that night. I thought he had used me. In a way, he had. But it hadn't been a lie. My dad, whose actions had changed the course of my life, wasn't guilty.

And if all that wasn't enough, I'd seen him myself. He saved my life and told me he was proud of me and then he left. And I'd never heard from him again.

What I wanted to say was that Neptune could have told me. He knew what I'd been through. He knew how I'd reacted when I lost my mom—the only person who meant anything to me at the time. I'd left her behind on Plunia to follow my dreams—illegally, thanks to my failed physical—and when the space pirates attacked, she was killed in the slaughter. I hated my dad so much that night. Neptune could have told me Jack Stryker wasn't responsible for what happened, and he didn't.

As I stood there staring at Neptune, I realized I'd never demanded an explanation. I'd never told him that I saw my dad on the trek to Venus. I'd spent the past two months living on a corner of Neptune's property, taking lessons from him that would further my education and someday remove the "space academy dropout" phrase that followed me around, generally trying to figure him out, but I'd avoided the inevitable confrontation that hung over us.

It was as if not talking about it kept me from thinking about my dad being locked up for decades while I'd done nothing about it.

As I stood in the dark, empty security section and locked eyes with Neptune, I knew I wasn't going to talk about it now either. Acknowledging my thoughts out loud was accepting that no matter how hard I tried to be good at my job, I'd failed at one very big thing. Protecting my family.

Based on the outcome of the trip to Venus, I couldn't say the same thing about Neptune. If anybody were keeping score on the matter, under "saved a family member," Neptune had a "1" and I had a big fat "0."

I closed my eyes and channeled my Plunian side. My dad's side. The cold, unemotional side. The side that focused on facts and data to make decisions. Not my heart. I opened my eyes and stared at Neptune. "Jack Stryker is a qualified choice. He lacks emotional attachment to Pika. He knows how to deal with space pirates. He flew our family spaceship to deliver dry ice so he's an experienced pilot. But we need someone who we can trust, and I don't think that's him."

"He's our only choice. I'll take responsibility for his actions." Neptune checked his watch. "You get one hour to explore the ship and find everything you need to know. Hack the database tonight. If anybody tries to contact Moon Unit, you can have the calls rerouted to the ship and I'll field them."

"Explore the ship? That feels like wasted time. We have a lot to do—"

"How well did you know Moon Unit 5 before departure? And Moon Unit 6?"

He had a point. Just because the company kept their schematics behind a password-protected firewall didn't mean I hadn't been able to access them. Thanks to my interest in knowing everything I could about the ships, I was probably more familiar with their layout than the architects who designed them.

"I can download the schematics while I'm in the database and study them tonight," I said.

"You've never had the opportunity to learn how a ship was laid out by experiencing it. Until now, you have only learned from illustrations." He crossed his arms.

"Consider this a teachable moment."

I crossed my arms too. We stood like that, facing each other in mimicked body language, for almost a minute. When I realized I was wasting valuable Moon Unit exploration time, I dropped my arms and left without saying a word.

It might have scared me how intuitive Neptune was with his lesson plan if not for one thing: I wanted to learn. In this case, he was right. I'd never walked the empty corridors of a spaceship. I had never had the chance to experience what it was like through the appearance, the scent, the touch of the ship. Each time I'd boarded one (which was exactly twice before today) I already had an idea of what to expect. It was like memorizing a black and white sketchbook and then being given the finished picture that someone else had colored in. But this time, I didn't start with a sketch. Every green carpet, every shiny white wall, every yellow railing that offered support alongside every curved hallway was new to me.

What I knew about Moon Unit Corporation was that they were a company who specialized in tourist travel to various destinations in the galaxy. The first three Moon Units had had their share of problems thanks to loose loyalties between departments. Moon Unit 4's fate was classified, and even my computer skills hadn't been able to expose what happened. I hacked my way onto a position on Moon Unit 5 and solved a murder, was a legitimate member of the crew of Moon Unit 6 and helped an escaped Venusian find freedom, but this time—this trek would be different. This time, I wasn't just along for the ride.

In reading the promotional material for Moon Unit Corp, I learned that they planned to diversify into smaller ships that could be chartered for privatized partying. The Moon Unit 7 Series seemed designed for that. The hallways were narrower than the last ship, and, aside from security section and engineering, everything was on the same flight deck. There was no upper floor or side quadrants. No need for high pressure transport to get from one side of the ship to the other. I could probably run end to end in under a minute.

I reached the front of the ship and stepped onto the bridge. In front of me, a curved fiberglass window stared out onto the docking station. When we took off, that screen would show nothing but black sky and stars. Our course would lead us past planets and asteroid fields, through meteors and moon dust. At the speeds Neptune said we'd be traveling probably none of us would get to see the sights. But they'd be there. The whole universe and then some would be there. Life on other planets. Maybe a girl staring up at the sky watching us fly past and saying to her dad, "someday that's going to be me."

I shook off the thought and left the bridge. Where had that come from? I didn't spend time thinking about those days. I was a different person now. This was my mission. I was in charge.

Okay, Neptune was in charge, but at least he let me think I had a say in the mission, and I appreciated that. But if I wanted his respect, I was going to have to show him I could do this. And technically speaking, if we were to default to my experience and his experience, there was one department where I *was* in charge. And it happened to be the one I was headed toward at the moment.

"Neptune? Can you hear me?"

"Go."

"Can't you just say, 'yes, hi Sylvia, I can hear you'?"

"Go."

"Meet me in the uniform ward immediately. There's one small matter we have to deal with before we even think about letting anybody else on this ship."

"What?"

"You. Your man-in-black thing. Not gonna fly if you're trying to pass yourself off as the captain." I paused to see if he was going to argue with me. When the pause felt long enough for him to have had an opportunity to argue the point and he didn't (for the record, seven tenths of a second seemed appropriate), I continued. "I'm outside the uniform ward right now. Get here as soon as you can."

"Stryker—"

I waved my hand in front of the door sensors and they swished open, revealing that Neptune had had the same thought as me.

To be honest, the open doors revealed more about Neptune than that.

7: ALL SYSTEMS GO

Neptune stood shirtless in front of the uniform closet. I stared at his expanse of bare chest. Broad shoulders, toned pecs, washboard abs. The man was a rock of muscle. His black cargo pants sat low on his hips, held in place with a military cotton web belt with a brushed chrome buckle. It took too long for me to realize I was staring at Neptune's belt buckle, which was in a general region that I (his mentee) probably shouldn't be staring. It took a few seconds after that to look away.

"Why didn't you tell me you were already here?" I asked. "I gave you seven tenths of a second."

He crossed his arms. "Seven tenths of a second is not enough time to allow the other party in your conversation to speak."

"Says who?"

"Common knowledge."

This was not the time for him to change the course

material. "Get out of the way," I said. "You don't know the organizational system."

"Neither do you. You've never been on Moon Unit Mini 7.2 before."

"No, but I memorized the BOP for the last two ships. How different could it be?"

The BOP—Book of Protocols—was essentially the bible for Moon Unit travel. The first time I memorized it, I'd been working from a copy I'd bought on the black market. The second time I'd gotten the legitimate one, all five hundred and twenty-three pages. Good thing I had a photographic memory.

Neptune stepped back and gave me access to the uniform closet. Regular crew uniforms filled the shelves in the front. It was a safe assumption that the job of the uniform lieutenant leaned heavily toward laundry services, but the occasional tear during flight meant we had to have backup inventory on hand to keep people in regulation. In addition to shelves of blue (medical staff), gray (flex crew), red (engineers and a few unlucky folks), and yellow (navigation), there was a secret compartment for top-level uniforms. I'd never needed to access them, but I knew they were there. I dropped to a squat, shifted the gray jerseys out of the way, and released the hidden door that contained the uniform I sought.

Any uniform I gave Neptune was going to have to be customized to fit. His muscular build wasn't exactly standard. And having now seen that build up close and personal, I recognized that there would be certain distractions that I hadn't yet encountered in my two previous shifts as uniform lieutenant. But I was a professional and this was part of my job.

I slid the desired uniform out of the compartment. It was a silver top and pants made from a durable fabric called Stealthyester®. The material was covered with tiny reflective surfaces that helped the wearer blend into his or her surroundings. It was also designed to block antigens and pathogens. The fabric wasn't yet approved for all crew members, but a special suit with automatic fit regulators was provided for the captain.

I handed the suit to Neptune.

His eyebrows pulled together, and three vertical lines appeared between them. "What's that?"

"Emergency captain suit. It's kept in reserve. It'll protect you against all kinds of threats. Take it. Put it on over your clothes. You'll want to have a buffer between the Stealthyester® and your skin." I tapped the customizers on the shoulder of the suit. "Once you have it on, press these to activate the fit sensors. The suit is self-altering to your build." Though, judging from the size of Neptune, the uniform was probably not going to have to do a whole lot of adjusting.

"What about you?"

"I was hired to test the next-gen uniforms by the supplier, remember? My suitcase is filled with things you only imagined. Not that you've imagined my uniforms. Or me in my uniforms." I shook my head to clear the distracting thoughts. "If there's one thing you don't need to worry about, it's what I'm going to wear."

Neptune studied me for another second. "Are you sure you can do this?" he asked.

A vision of the message that Cat had projected against the exterior of Mattix's ship flashed into my memory. Pika in trouble. Mattix dead. Them turning to me to help. Me needing Neptune's experience to make it happen.

"Yes," I said. It wasn't the time for a flip answer.

"Go to security section and contact your crew. I'll be busy with pre-flight checks all night. The next time you see me will be departure."

***

Twelve hours later, the ship was staffed with a skeleton crew. Lt. Ivi, a petite, green Martian woman, was assigned to communications. Martians had cornered the communications industry thanks to their skills in memorizing hundreds of languages and dialects through the galaxy. This would be my first time working with a female Martian.

Kentaro was our medic. Military trained but sustained an injury in the line of duty. Whatever medical emergencies he couldn't handle, his robot, T-Fal, could. According to Kentaro's application, T-Fal was made from non-stick cookware that had been found in a landfill on

Earth. The Teflon-coated aluminum was a surprisingly resilient material that allowed the robot to withstand high temperatures and double as a short order cook in Kentaro's military unit. When the medic was released from active duty, he'd taken T-Fal with him to ease his transition into daily life.

I'd left the details of my dad's arrival to Neptune. I assumed he was on the ship somewhere, but that wasn't my problem. Neptune hadn't questioned my suggestion that we divide and conquer the crew arrivals and, while I suspected he knew my motivation, I secretly appreciated him not asking point blank.

I hadn't been able to reach our previous engineer and had put out a call on a security message board. It had been a risky move since the message could be visible to anyone looking at the postings on the job board after hours. I gambled that I could delete the posting as soon as the job was filled. Anybody who claimed to have seen it wouldn't be able to prove it, making them look bad while giving us the time we needed to blast off.

The crew member to fill that position was Rebel Rune. A local man, he showed up with a copy of his medical papers, a surprising knowledge of Moon Unit Corporation, and a letter of recommendation from Federation Council.

I activated the sequence that closed and sealed the ship for departure. The door eased down from above to close and then stopped. White lights blinked, and a computerized voice said, "Obstruction. Door cannot close. Obstruction. Door cannot close. Obstruction. Door cannot close. Obstruction—"

I stepped away from the door and hit the interrupt command button. A blue bag, bulging with medical gear, turned out to be the obstruction. Boots were visible next to the bag, and from the position of the boots, I'd go so far as to say someone was wearing them. I undid the sequence in the control panel and the door lifted, leaving me face to face with Doc Edison.

"Sylvia," he said, surprised. "I didn't expect to find you here."

"Doc—hi—I—um—" In terms of acting normal, I was doing a poor job. "I thought you weren't available for this trek." I bent down and grabbed the handles of his medical bag. "Come on in. I was about to seal the ship."

He looked suspicious. "Darn computer scheduling system. Nothing works like it's supposed to. We need to go back to the way they did things on Earth. Write stuff on a calendar. Check it daily."

"Your scheduler malfunctioned?" This time I was suspicious.

He shook his head. "Somehow the scheduler put Moon Unit 7.2 into next month instead of this one. I would have missed it if the new engineer hadn't contacted me for an emergency physical."

"Lieutenant Rune?"

Doc nodded. "Nice kid. Comes highly recommended.

I'm surprised we haven't heard much about him before."

So was I. And with the rumble of the thrusters igniting beneath my feet, I recognized that any investigation into Rebel Rune's background was going to have to be done in flight. While I kept Doc so busy in Medi-Bay that he wouldn't have a chance to find out what we were really up to.

An untested engineer. A suspicious doctor. A hijacked ship. And a secret rescue mission that depended heavily on the skill set of a man who'd been in jail while I'd gone through puberty. We'd stacked the deck with jokers and now we needed passengers to keep Doc busy.

At least I had a pretty good idea where to find them.

8: TRANSPORT TROUBLE

Moon Unit Mini 7.2 departed the docking station without fanfare. More possibly, any fanfare connected to the departure of Moon Unit Mini 7.2 came after we were past the breakaway point and the powers that be discovered the ship was missing. My hope was that by the time we returned, we'd be viewed as heroes and not thieves. Stealing a spaceship was probably punishable by a pretty hefty sentence and I had no intentions of following in my dad's footsteps when it came to things like that.

My dad. Memories and suppositions about him popped into my head at the least desired times. I knew he was going to be on this mission. Neptune was handling that. Which meant at any given moment I could round a corner and be face to face with the man who most of the galaxy believed was a criminal. I could handle the skeleton crew, the unknown engineer, the presence of Doc, and the mission to save Pika. But I didn't know how

I'd handle seeing dad.

At least there was no time to think about that now. Indicator lights on the walls clicked on, signaling the ship's breathable air was at a stable level. I switched off my oxygen tank and set my bubble helmet on the floor next to Neptune's security section computer. Underneath the desk was a button that switched us from the main network to the dark web. I cloned the first five security sign-in measures including the spinning Moon Unit logo and created a fake flight plan. If anybody got suspicious about what we were doing, this was the first thing they'd check. I couldn't keep them from following their instincts to make sure we were on the up and up. All I could do was fake the information they'd find and make sure it gave away nothing of our agenda.

From the docking station, it was about 2.5 billion miles to Saturn. On the way, we'd fly through the M-13, a stretch of the galaxy under Federation Council rule. We needed an honest-to-goodness reason for being there, and there was only one that would be plausible. We were picking up our passengers.

Of the thirteen colonies in the M-13, two stood out. Colony 7 and Colony 13. Colony 13 was where convicted criminals were kept. It was illegal to pick up passengers from there.

But Colony 7 was where Gremlons like Pika lived. Their elders had made a case to Federation Council to provide them with a place to live in peace. Since relocating the race of goofy pink aliens to Colony 7, their lifespan had increased exponentially. As it turned out, they were worthless as slaves and unreliable as employees. When a Gremlon got scared, they shrunk in size. When a Gremlon got *really* scared, they curled up into a ball and sometimes stayed that way until they died. It was considered an epidemic, which was why Federation Council agreed with the elders.

What was particularly beneficial to us was that Federation Council also agreed to limit communications to Colony 7. It would have been too easy to exploit the flibbertigibbet nature of Gremlons by those with ulterior motives, so communications to the planet either passed through FC operators or were broadcast publicly. The belief was that no one would broadcast a malicious message to the public, and that belief had turned out to be true.

And it was also why I'd planted an ad on the Colony 7 Broadcast Network for free passes aboard Moon Unit Mini 7.2 to the first five Gremlons who showed up to the transport coordinates listed in the ad. Neptune would use those coordinates to land the ship on Colony 7, board the five winners, and take off. We'd be back in zero gravity before anybody outside the colony knew what had happened.

Gremlons were a handful, but I was pretty sure I could handle five of them. If they were anything like Pika, I could set them up in Ion-54, aim the rotating light device at the multifaceted silver orb suspended over the dance floor, and leave. Gremlons *loved* sparkly things.

"Lieutenant Stryker to bridge," I said. The one thing Neptune and I hadn't worked out was how we were going to communicate in public.

"Go."

Okay, we were going to communicate like usual. "Request meeting in Council Chambers."

"Go."

"I don't know if anybody else can hear me and I think it's best if we have a meeting alone in Council Chambers."

"Stryker. Until we have a navigator, I'm alone on the bridge. You can make your report now or you can come to the bridge, but until there's someone else to take over, I'm not going anywhere."

"I'll be right there."

I switched off the computer and went to the bridge. The doors swished open when I arrived, but this time, it wasn't the view of outer space that made me speechless. It was Neptune in the silver Stealthyester® custom-fitted uniform.

"You look like a captain," I said, a little breathless. "Good job."

"I should say that to you. You're the uniform lieutenant."

"About that. Considering we only have a limited crew, doesn't it seem weird to have a uniform lieutenant? I mean, come on. Captain, medic, engineer, communicator...and uniform lieutenant?"

"Uniform ward is under the security wing. You're a security officer." His eyes shifted to my green uniform. "You need to change."

"I'm testing this one. It's made out of rubber. Watch." I swung my arms in circles. Neptune reached a fist out and caught my wrist. "You get the point." I walked past him and pointed to the captain's chair. "How come you're not sitting?"

"Make your report, Stryker."

Neptune doesn't want to sit in the captain's chair. The thought hit me like a laser blast between the eyes. He was doing what he had to do to make this mission work just like I was. But that didn't mean he didn't have his own demons.

The thought made me stand a little straighter. This was no joke. The outcome of this trek could change both of our lives in ways I hadn't begun to imagine.

"Our flight plan has been entered into the database. Crew members are in position. Two potential threats: Rebel Rune answered the call for an engineer. There was no time to run a thorough check into his background."

Neptune nodded once. "And two?"

"Lieutenant Rune contacted Doc Edison to clear him for travel. Doc assumed his scheduler made a mistake and he showed up at the docking station."

"He's here? On the ship?"

"Yes, and I'm pretty sure he's already suspicious. He might turn us in when we get to Colony 7."

"Change in plans," Neptune said. He approached the navigation panel and moved his finger about the colorful display. "What are the coordinates you put in the broadcast to the Gremlons?"

I recited the numbers from memory. Neptune keyed them in and activated the communication channel to engineering. "Bridge to engineering. Prepare to rematerialize five Gremlons from the following coordinates." He read off the numbers.

I held my breath. We had one shot in using the materializer to pick up the Gremlons, and it would only work if they were exactly where I'd told them to be. Bundles of energy that they were, my hopes of them standing still were not high. "Activate."

There was silence on the other end of the communicator. And then cursing. And then more cursing. And then an apology, and then Rune said, "I'm going to need some help down here."

Neptune and I looked at each other. A highly recommended graduate from Space Academy with an engineering background should be able to handle five Gremlons without a lot of effort.

"What's the problem?" Neptune asked.

"I thought you said five."

"I did."

"Then the machine must have malfunctioned. There are about fifty of these pink things down here and they're going crazy!"

9: THINK PINK

I was out the door before Neptune could stop me. Into the stairwell, down to engineering, to the transport deck—holy moly!

There were Gremlons everywhere. Pale pink, skinny aliens with pointy ears. Some were curled into balls. Others backed up against the wall. A couple hugged each other and looked around, wide-eyed. And Lt. Rune was crouched in the corner with his hands over his eyes, peeking through his fingers.

"Rune," I said. "What happened?"

"I switched on the materializer and they started showing up. Tons of them. I switched the device off, but they were already here. I don't know what happened. I swear I did what they taught me at the academy."

I held out a hand and pulled him to his feet. "I think I know what happened and it wasn't your fault." It was mine. I'd offered free trips to the first five Gremlons in line. They'd piled on top of each other to be those first five. The materializer had picked up the Gremlons that should have been in those positions. And it did. A lot more of them than I expected.

Too bad I hadn't had the foresight to include an entertainment director in our crew.

I turned to Rune. "Activate the emergency lights." Rune looked scared. I reached past him and slapped my hand on the button that flashed the Code White through the ship. Considering how few of us there were, I assumed everybody would remember Code White was not a threat and would continue doing what they were doing. Neptune would see the lights and know where I was.

As I'd hoped, the Gremlons saw the lights blinking around the perimeter of the room and quieted down. The ones that were balled up slowly uncurled themselves. They chattered in high pitched voices and stared while the pulse flickered.

"They like flashing lights and sparkly things. The lights will keep them entertained for a while. I'll send Doc to check them out and make sure nothing happened to them when they, um, arrived."

"You mean they could die?" Rune's face fell. "Like that one?"

"Which one?" I turned around and saw a grey alien face down by the far wall of the transport deck. A grey alien like the one that had gotten off Mattix's space pod. My heartbeat picked up and my palms got sweaty.

"Where'd he come from?"

"He showed up with the others," Rune said. "I thought maybe he was dirty."

"He's a grey." Grey Two, I added to myself, taking note of the number on his hand. I climbed onto the transport deck and walked up to the alien. Around me, the Gremlons chattered. They had a habit of repeating words three times, and with fifty of them speaking at the same time, the result was impossible to understand. But when I looked up at their faces, I knew they were waiting to see what I'd do to the grey. To me, he was a threat. To them, he was a passenger who'd shown up on Moon Unit 7.2 the same way they had. If I nudged his hand and it disintegrated, they'd assume that's what I'd do to them too.

I backed away from the alien. "Notify Doc. Tell him—" I scanned the faces of the Gremlons again—"tell him you have a whole lot of passengers who need medical attention and one who requires containment. He'll know what to do when he gets here."

I left engineering and went back to security section. Next to my belongings, still waiting to be moved to my quarters, sat Cat. All this started when I'd activated his data panel and heard the message from Pika.

I flipped Cat over and turned on the replay feature. His eyes lit up and the cone of digital data projected upside down onto the brick wall at the back of the holding cell. I flipped him again and aimed him at a smoother wall and sank down onto the cot to watch Pika's message again.

"Now you be a good cat, okay? Go get Sylvia and tell her we need her help. But don't tell the giant. If he finds out I went to Saturn, he'll be mad mad mad. I know Sylvia kept my secret. She promised. Bye-bye, Cat."

I stared at the wall after the image went to black. This was all my fault. I knew Pika was going to Saturn and I knew it was a bad idea. I knew it so much that I'd let her take Cat and I'd taught her how to use him to record a message. And she was such a sweet thing that she sent him back—the one thing that could have kept her company—because she needed help.

The period of inactivity after Pika's message ended triggered Cat's power-saver mode. A cooling fan inside him whirred, and he tipped forward as his front legs buckled in, and then lowered to the ground. His back legs followed suit. He'd switch to sleep mode in five minutes if I left him there and would wake up the next time bright light hit his sensors. But this was security section and it was dark (something I knew from the time Neptune arrested me). I stood and picked Cat off the floor.

He woke back up. The fan stopped, and his eyes lit up again. Had Pika not remembered how to turn his recorder off? That could mean a lot of things, including him not having as much internal blank space for future files as I thought.

Or it could mean something else.

This time I kept Cat on my lap and aimed him at the wall next to me. A projection showed two grey aliens walking side by side across a lunar surface. The body of a man in cobalt blue Federation Council robes lay prone. The greys grabbed his ankles and slowly dragged him across Cat's sight line. They stopped when the body was in the center of the frame and aimed vaporizers at him. A beam of electric yellow came out of the nozzle of the vaporizer, cast an outline over the man, and then he disappeared. A third man entered the frame—a grungy space pirate with long, matted hair and spindly arms and legs. I'd seen his picture enough times to recognize him even though I'd never met him face to face. Omicron Faarstar.

Had Pika known she was recording this? Had she intended for me to find evidence that the greys, under the instruction of a known space pirate, had vaporized a member of Federation Council? Or had she recorded this by accident? If she had done it intentionally, did they know she took the video? And since it was after the message she had programmed for me, was it an afterthought or had she caught this action first, and then accidentally recorded over it with her call for help?

There was something more troubling about the images Cat projected. The grey aliens. One grey, I could have written off as a hitchhiker through the galaxy. Two, maybe a coincidence. But this projection told me it was no coincidence. The dead grey that had transported in with the Gremlons tied everything together. I just didn't know how.

I radioed to Medi-Bay. "Doc? It's Sylvia. I mean Lieutenant Stryker."

"What kind of an idiot thought it was a good idea to fill a miniature Moon Unit with Gremlons?" he answered. "This company has some wacky ideas for publicity."

"Are they going to be okay?"

"They'll survive. Gremlons have a pretty simplified physiological makeup so there's not much to scramble when they get zapped through space. Now me? I'm perfectly fine traveling the old-fashioned way."

"What about the dead one? Were you able to contain him?"

"You must have been wrong about that. There was no dead one. Rune said the one you thought was dead must have just been stunned. He got up and walked out with the rest of them."

My internal radar that sensed trouble was off the charts. "Doc, did you check out all of them? The Gremlons?"

"Yep. All forty-seven of them."

"And they're okay?"

"Yep. A little on the nervous side but they'll snap out of it."

"How's their coloring?"

"What do you mean? They're pink. The whole lot of them is the color of the soap Moon Unit Corporation uses in the lavatories."

"You're sure?"

"I don't know if you're insulting my medical abilities or my vision."

"Neither. Thanks, Doc. Stryker out."

If I thought things were bad before, they'd just gotten worse. We had a grey alien stowaway on board Moon Unit 7.2, and I had evidence that the greys were responsible for Mattix's death.

10: MORE FUN THAN A BARREL OF MONKEYS

I removed a tiny toolkit from my backpack and unscrewed the panel that held Cat's data chip. Neptune needed to see what I'd found.

A burst of static filled my ear. "Where are you?" Neptune asked.

"Security section. I found something on Cat that you need to see."

"I'll take your report after you meet Doc in Medi-Bay. He's got his hands full with the Gremlons."

"No! This is an emergency."

The comm was silent. I'd never yelled at Neptune before. I'd never flat-out refused an order, and him being in charge of both my off-the-books education and my on-the-ship safety, I may have just made a major overstep.

"Go."

See? That told me nothing. "In addition to the forty-seven Gremlons that were transported onto the ship, we picked up a grey. I thought he was dead when I saw him face down on the transport pad, but Doc said Rune told him he got up and left."

"Greys will play dead to fool their attacker. Did you nudge him?"

"No. The Gremlons were skittish and I thought if they saw me disintegrate a grey in front of them, they'd see me as a threat, and once that happened, I'd never win them over."

"Good call. Did Rune see anything?"

"That's the thing. Rune told Doc it was a Gremlon."

"How sure are you that it was a grey?"

"I know the difference between grey and pink, Neptune. I'm not colorblind."

"Greys don't. To them, you're not purple. You look just like me."

"Somebody needs to give them the diversity memo." I flipped the data chip over between my fingers. "I'm scared, Neptune. I found more data on the chip in Cat, and it shows two greys vaporizing a Federation Council member twice their size. Pika either saw it happen or set Cat up to record it."

"That doesn't sound like something she'd do. Put that data chip somewhere safe and get to Medi-Bay. I'll review it with you as soon as the ship goes on auto-pilot."

"Okay. Stryker out."

I closed my hand around the data chip. Now that I knew how important it was to protect it, I couldn't think of a decent hiding place.

The image of Pika talking to Cat and asking me for help wouldn't seem so innocent to the Gremlons on the ship. They were already scared, and they'd see that as Pika being held captive.

I also knew if Grey Two vaporized me while I had the chip, it would be disintegrated. Important intel needed to be isolated. Neptune knew that I knew that, and the first thing he'd do would be to search my last known location.

Which wouldn't do a whole lot for me, but it would help the greater good. Maybe moving it was the mistake. I slipped it back into Cat and left.

I arrived in Medi-Bay a few minutes later. There were Gremlons everywhere. Doc held a wand with a flashing blue light and moved back and forth between a row of beds. The pink aliens watched the wand with wide eyes. They didn't even notice me enter.

"Sylvia. Thank god. Grab a glow stick and wave it at these things." He tipped his head back toward a pile of party sticks on the table.

"Do I want to know why you have glow sticks in bulk?"

"No. You don't."

I grabbed a couple of the flexible tubes and bent them until the radium caplet inside broke and they illuminated. The Gremlons close to me reached out to touch and I pulled the glowing sticks out of their reach.

"What do you want me to do with them?"

"I don't know. Entertain them? Distract them? I've only cleared about half of them for travel. So far, they're fine but I'm not going to take a chance. Rune said one was a little pale and without being able to examine him, I can't predict his condition."

"Did Rune say anything else?"

Doc turned his attention from the Gremlon to me. "No. Why?"

"No reason."

He shined his light directly into my eyes and I blinked several times. "Lieutenant Stryker, what is going on? Why are there fifty Gremlons on this ship?"

"Forty-seven. They're our passengers. We're taking them to Saturn."

"How did Gremlons afford to charter a Moon Unit?" He kept the light trained on my pupil.

"It was a prize. Publicity, like you said."

"This is a Moon Unit Mini. Comfortably sleeps twenty-five and that includes the crew. Whoever promised safe passage to all these Gremlons needs to have their head checked."

One thing was clear. Doc didn't believe a word I said. And worse, he was using classic interrogation techniques to catch me in a lie. I did the one thing that would get him off my back. I confessed.

"That would be me."

"You?"

"It's a training mission, okay?" A full confession seemed counterproductive, so I embellished. "That's why you didn't have it on your schedule. The crew is being tested to see how they'd do on a real moon trek. Everything is a simulation."

Doc squinted and held the light steady. I knew that by telling the truth, my pupils would change shape, my temperature would drop, my pulse would slow. All signs that he could believe me. Just because I withheld a couple of details didn't mean I wasn't telling the truth.

"A training mission?" he asked. I nodded. "That makes sense. Moon Unit Corp has been expanding. They need a second unit team. And these mini-ships won't require the same level of experience or staff as the old ones. It's not a bad idea. You said it was yours?"

I nodded again.

"Not bad," he said again. He switched off the light. It would take a while for my vision to return in that eye. "Well, if a bunch of Gremlons is the worst thing I have to manage while we're traveling, I can do that. Tell you what. I know you've been through a lot and I want to help you succeed. I'll take responsibility for these pink things. Go back out to the ship and see what you can do to help the captain."

"Thanks, Doc."

I turned around to leave and got halfway to the door when he asked, "Speaking of which, who is the captain? Anybody I know?"

The answer to Doc's question would have to wait. The doors to Medi-Bay swished open and Neptune entered with a purple man who, by all accounts, was a stranger to me.

My dad.

11: FATHER FIGURE

Jack Stryker had once been respected throughout the galaxy. As the main exporter of dry ice to neighboring planets of Plunia, he maintained friendly relations with everyone he met, thus currying favor among his contacts. If Plunia held elections like they had on Earth, my dad would have been a favored candidate. Which was why it was such a surprise—and a knife to the heart—when the news broke that he'd turned on his planet and sold them out to space pirates.

The stories varied in nature, but the gist was this: my dad had enlisted the help of the evil space pirate Cheung Qidd to destroy competitors' dry ice mines to drive up the value of the ice balls mined by him and my mom. The act made him a small fortune that had never been found. He was arrested and tried by Federation Council, where twenty-two out of twenty-three council members voted to banish him to Colony 13. The remaining member didn't so much as believe in my dad's innocence as in the possible repercussions of a guilty vote. At the time he'd been my boyfriend. Vaan Marshall.

Vaan's recusal from the vote didn't sit all that well with me, especially since Vaan was the only Plunian on the Council. We broke up. My dad went to jail. I dropped out of school and devoted my life to helping my mom establish a reputation not tied to my dad. It was an uphill battle. Not only because she'd had the bad foresight to marry a traitor, but because my mom was from Earth. Two strikes.

And then there was me. Half Plunian. Half Earthling. High school dropout. No matter what achievements and accolades I'd accrued while at the academy, now I was nothing but trash. One by one, even my friends stopped hanging around.

I'd had my dad to blame for all of it. And then two months ago, I found out it was a lie. People I trusted said Jack Stryker was working on the inside.

If I hadn't heard it from Neptune and confirmed with a Plunian Moon Unit captain, I might not have believed it myself. It sure would have been easier to keep on hating him.

And now he was here. On the ship. Helping Neptune and me save a scared Gremlon and avenge a space courier's murder.

"Lieutenant Stryker," the man said formally. Like the last time I'd seen him, for a brief moment on board Moon

Unit 6, I felt who he was without requiring proof. He was purple like all Plunians, had a thick head of hair and a full beard, and bright green eyes the shade of poisonous chlorine gas. He was taller than I was but shorter than Neptune, and his frame, hidden under loose robes, seemed on the wiry side. When I was young and watched him load his delivery ship, I told him he didn't look strong enough to lift the dry ice balls. I still remember what he'd said: strength doesn't come from muscles. It comes from within.

He stepped forward. Neptune put out his arm to block him. Doc stepped closer to me. I was rooted to the floor with a fist full of glow sticks.

"Is somebody going to tell me what the heck is going on?" Doc said. None of us answered. Doc looked Neptune up and down. "What are you wearing?"

"He's testing a prototype safety suit with improved flexibility," I said.

To Neptune's credit, he didn't flinch. I thought about asking him to demonstrate with some lunges, but the moment didn't seem right.

Doc seemed more interested in Jack than in Neptune's captain's uniform. "Have we met before? You look familiar."

Neptune spoke. "Doc, this is Jack. He's our navigator. He needs a full physical."

Doc's brows pulled together. "In case you haven't noticed, I have my hands full with our special guests." He waved an open palm around Medi-Bay to indicate the Gremlons.

The quiet Gremlons. A hush had come over them. As I looked from round pink face to round pink face, I saw awe reflected at me. Doc saw it too. He turned from the Gremlons to me. "Stand still," he instructed. He held his thermometer by my temple and whistled. "Your temp is off the charts."

"She's Plunian," my dad said.

"Half Plunian," I corrected not looking at him. "My core temperature is around a hundred and twenty degrees."

"You're about to climb over one-thirty-five and I don't care what color your skin is, when your temperature gets over one thirty, you become a danger to yourself. From what you've told me, we can't afford to have a crew member down."

"I'll give her a physical," my dad said.

"Absolutely not!" I said.

My dad continued to address Doc as if I hadn't said a word. "I'm familiar with Plunian core temperatures and the easiest ways to bring them down. I understand you're a student of Hale Williams's methods. I studied his principles while at my last assignment."

I stared at Neptune. Why wasn't he interrupting? He knew how I felt. Why wasn't he using his leverage as acting captain to reiterate his order, make Doc do the physical on my dad and then me, and leave?

Neptune didn't do anything without a plan. I *hated* when Neptune had a plan that I didn't know! We were so going to talk about that later.

I'd studied tactical advantage before leaving school and I could figure this out. But it wasn't the point of our mission and it wasn't why we'd hijacked a ship. Until we reached Saturn, there was one objective and we couldn't achieve our objective if Doc reported us.

"I was trained on Dr. Hale Williams's methodology too," Neptune said. We all stared at him. "I'll treat Lieutenant Stryker. Doc, run a physical on Jack. I need him back on the bridge by Zulu Five."

Doc was surprised. I was relieved. Jack was angry, and his anger was directed at Neptune.

Interesting.

Neptune grabbed my arm and led me to his quarters. Unlike the asylum gray shade of his room on the last Moon Unit, this time he'd moved into the suite designed for the captain. And even for a Moon Unit Mini Series 7, it was spacious.

He opened a cabinet and pulled out a box of Mars Bars. "Eat."

"Are you kidding?"

"There's no restaurant on the ship. Eat."

I grabbed a bar and tore off the wrapper. Neptune pressed a button on the wall and a red light went on over the door.

"You have one of those too?" I asked after I

swallowed. "I guess you would. Is the room soundproof? We can talk without the risk of someone hearing us?"

"Go."

"There's a grey loose on the ship. He came on with the Gremlons and played dead. Rune either knows or is an idiot. He told Doc I was wrong."

"Objective assessment: could you have been wrong?"

"No."

"Any idea what he wants?"

"No, but considering a grey hitched to your place on Mattix's pod and Cat recorded a video of greys vaporizing a Federation Council member, I think it's all connected."

"Risk?"

"High. We have six crew members counting us, two robots, a suspicious doctor, forty-seven Gremlons, and an unknown number of possibly hostile grey aliens on the ship. And I'm running a fever."

"You're not running a fever."

"You heard Doc."

"Doc's infrared thermometer picked up the combined reading of you and your dad. He only noticed because you started to glow. Didn't you see how the Gremlons looked at you?"

"What about my dad? Why did you ask Doc to run a physical on him?"

"Doc is our wildcard. He said Jack looked familiar and it's only a matter of time until he figures out why. None of us know what he's going to do when that happens. He needs to discover the truth and do whatever it is he thinks is right. Once we know his intended actions, we'll be able to formulate a plan."

It made sense. It was smart.

It was risky too, but we didn't have time to play things safe.

"I thought I only glowed around you," I said. Neptune raised one eyebrow. "You know what I mean. The trip to Venus. You told me that planet made me turbocharged."

"We're nowhere near Venus. The condition was triggered by your reaction to seeing your dad. There's nothing wrong with you."

After a lifetime of wondering if there was, the words sounded surprisingly refreshing. "Thank you," I said. "I know it wasn't a compliment, but—"

Neptune stepped forward and tipped my chin up. The warm buzz that I'd felt through my body when we were on the trip to Venus returned. I didn't have to look at my arms to know I was glowing.

The ship jerked. I lost my balance and fell against Neptune. I quickly regained my footing and stepped away. He put his hand out on the wall. More turbulence. His bags, bulging with whatever equipment he'd packed on the ship, vibrated off the table and fell onto the floor.

"Something's wrong," he said. He ran out the door and headed toward the bridge with me hot on his heels.

12: STRUCTURAL DAMAGE

Neptune burst onto the bridge and called engineering. "Rune, what's happening?"

"We hit an asteroid field, captain. The navigator must have plotted a bad course. I'm doing what I can, but at this speed, we're getting knocked around like a tetherball."

"What if we go to warp?"

I grabbed Neptune's arm. "We're not supposed to go to warp until tonight. When everybody is asleep."

Rune cursed over the intercom.

"What?" Neptune asked.

"One of our fuel rods just separated from the ship. Who cleared this thing for travel?"

Nobody had cleared the ship for travel. We assumed all along that the ship we stole was ready for action. It was the first of too many risky assumptions, but there was no going back now.

Neptune turned off the intercom. "What would you do?" he asked me.

"We need to plot a new course and go to warp sooner than we expected. We have to get past the asteroid field," I said.

"Do you understand the risks?"

"The only risk is not saving Pika. That's the mission. At this rate the ship is going to fall apart before we reach Saturn. Warp is the only responsible choice."

Something crashed into the side of the ship and sent us both flying. Neptune returned to the side of the captain's chair and pressed the communication button. "Attention. This is your captain. We've encountered an unexpected asteroid field which is causing turbulence. We're going to warp to minimize damage to the ship. Prepare for increased speed in sixty seconds."

He released the button. "Go to your quarters, Stryker."

"I'm not leaving the bridge," I said.

Another hit. This time I fell. I pulled myself up, bent over the closest computer screen, and accessed the feed from the cameras on the exterior of the ship. I should have seen debris or asteroid dust. Maybe the cameras would have been damaged. But there was nothing of the sort. The cameras picked up the blackness of space, peppered only with floating particles that glistened with the reflection of our exterior lights.

I studied the flight plan. We were on the same course

I'd plotted from the uniform ward. There were no asteroids in our way, on our side, or anywhere around us. Whatever was beating up the ship had nothing to do with exterior elements. It was a trap.

"Call off the warp command," I said.

"Why?"

"The visual screens should have confirmed Rune's report and they didn't. There's nothing out there. There's nothing visible on the exterior ship cameras. Someone wants us to go to warp, but if we do, the ship will fall apart."

"How sure are you?"

"One hundred percent."

Neptune flipped the plastic bubble off the switch to cancel his recent command. We locked eyes. I had no idea what number the countdown was on, but I didn't look away. He pressed the button.

"Warp command canceled," said a computerized female voice. "Systems returning to previously chartered speed and course."

I looked at the screen. Three seconds left. I held my breath and waited for another blow to the ship. None came. What did it mean?

I spun back around. Neptune was behind the captain's chair with his hands on it. His jaw was clenched, and his brows were hooded over his eyes. His anger was palpable. And then it hit me. Going to warp had been my call. He asked what I would have done, and I told him. It led to almost certain death. Someone had played us. They'd played me. So much for teachable moments.

I stood up. "I was wrong. And I was out of line. I take full responsibility. Maybe I don't have what it takes to do what you do." I waited for him to say something. I knew he was a man of few words, but if ever he were going to break out of his old habits and prove that something—anything—I'd ever said to him had changed him even in the slightest, now was the time.

He didn't.

I left the bridge in silence and spent the night in the uniform ward. From the moment we departed, the trip to Saturn had been full-speed ahead and there hadn't been time to select quarters and unpack my things which were still in security section. Plunians didn't require a lot of sleep, but I managed to catch a couple of hours of rest.

***

The next morning when I woke, I changed into a fresh uniform and sorted through the inventory. I'd made a risky, wrong decision and had almost gotten us all killed. We'd been foolish to think we could hijack a Moon Unit and fly a rescue mission with an untested crew. In a prototype ship. With an escaped convict-slash-father figure on board.

What made me think we could do this? Why did I always think I was smarter than everybody else?

The answer was simple. I knew what it felt like when everybody thought they were smarter than I was, and I'd developed a distorted sense of confidence as a defense mechanism. Fat lot of good that did me now. The sudden change in speed had loosened the fuel rod. We were on a ship that probably hadn't passed the safety inspection, gliding on a lackadaisical path toward Saturn. If we got there before the next light year, it would be a miracle.

I pulled all of the XS and S uniforms out of the closet and stuffed them into bags. The Gremlons might as well have something to wear for the duration of the trip. I'd set them up in guest quarters and spend my time making new friends. I didn't expect Neptune to give me any more opportunities to make the wrong decision.

I secured the uniform ward and rode the elevator to the lower level to get my things. I strapped on my backpack, grabbed Cat, and walked down the hallway to the staircase. Voices in engineering caught my attention.

Voices. More than one. I hid behind a wall and listened.

"She told him to put the ship into warp," one voice said. "They were three seconds away from destruction."

My skin flushed hot. I hadn't spent enough time with our crew to recognize the speakers, but whoever it was knew the decision to go to warp was mine. But why'd they say "they" and not "we?" Whoever it was would have been destroyed too.

I set my things down and prepared to confront whoever it was if only to shut down the gossip. But when I looked around the wall, I changed my mind.

It wasn't anyone from our crew. It was a pair of grey

aliens.

13: TRAITORS 'R US

There was no mistaking what I saw. Their bulbous heads and spindly bodies were easy to recognize. The two silhouettes appeared to be having a friendly conversation in the engineering quadrant. About the ship almost falling apart. After I told Neptune to go to warp.

Except technically, Rune was the one who'd suggested warp first. Rune who worked down here in engineering. He was the one who said we were in an asteroid field. He said if we continued to let the asteroids pummel us, the damage would be irreparable. He'd gone so far as to say we'd lost a fuel rod. How could I check to see if we'd lost a fuel rod?

I could ask Neptune, but I wouldn't. I'd lost all credibility with him.

I could ask my dad, but I wouldn't. Maybe everybody else was willing to believe he was a good guy, but I wasn't sure yet. And if he wasn't, my asking would only give him more power over us.

I could suit up in a thermal, open-atmosphere protective suit, climb into the repair hatch, tether myself to the safety hook, and float out to check it myself. I *could* do that, but I didn't want to.

I could run diagnostics. Yes!

There were two computers that would be safe to use to access that info. Security section, which was right down the hall, and the uniform ward. I'd sealed the uniform ward and reentry would alert Neptune. And until I had information to redeem myself, I wanted to stay hidden.

I crept through the hallway to security section and activated the computer. I hacked past the firewall to Moon Unit Corp (somebody needed to teach the system moderators to change their passwords once in a while) to the library of ship designs. I opened the folder, pulled up the plans for the Moon Unit Mini Series, and used an illustrator program to mock up a 3-D rotating view of Moon Unit Mini 7.2.

Once I located the fuel rods, I accessed the data logs and ran diagnostics on that section of the ship. The report came back clear. I ran a separate diagnostic report on the whole ship. It came back clear too.

Whatever had caused the turbulence and the direct hits hadn't done anything more than cause false panic. Which had probably been the goal.

How perfect of a plan that must have been. Employ an exterior force to create the illusion of damage. Have a member of the crew confirm the damage. Sit back and let the crew make decisions which would destroy the ship before we reached our destination. No shots fired. No evidence of attack. Just a ship that fell apart because a crew made a decision that turned out to be wrong. It suggested that whoever was responsible had that as their endgame. And if it was, they probably had an escape plan for themselves.

They.

The intel we'd acted on was fake.

There was one problem with that. Why would Rune have allowed the ship to be disintegrated while he was on it?

My thoughts were interrupted by the sound of a cat. *My* Cat. Meowing. From the hallway where I'd left him.

I dropped onto my knees and peered past the computer toward Engineering. The contents of my backpack would give away my identity, no doubt. And Cat had the data chip from Pika. If we lost that, we'd be done.

The corridor was dark and sterile. Dull black floors provided little in the way of reflective shadows. In the main part of the ship, the walls were built from fiberglass, used for both its durability and weightless properties. They were molded into undulating curves in a former government fabrication factory and fitted inside the shell of the Moon Unit that ships architects had designed. All the style that was advertised in the promotional catalogs was on the floor above me. Down here, everything had a purpose and the purpose was to make the inhabitant of the holding cell uncomfortable.

A beam of light bounced around the hallway. There and gone. There and gone. The movement of the light beam marked the location of the approaching greys that I'd overheard. They were trying to figure out which way I had gone. The light must have hit Cat because he meowed again. He was closer to me than to the stairs. The light got brighter and moved in my direction. I had no weapon. No place to hide. Nowhere to go. *Crap!*

"Sylvia, come out and play…" said a voice. Creepy laughter followed.

Whoever was there knew who I was. If I could lure them into the holding cell, I could activate the beams that served as bars and detain them until I could get help. But I didn't know how to lure them without being in the cell myself, and if I was in the cell, I wouldn't be able to activate the beams. This loner stuff was hard.

A burst of static sounded in my ear. The comm device! Oh. The comm device. Neptune could hear me, but I couldn't talk. If I spoke, I'd give away my presence. I'd get vaporized before I got out a word. And if I stood there, I'd get an earful about having almost gotten us disintegrated. And then Neptune's voice spoke. "I'm behind you. Stand up. Let them see you. Get their attention then drop back down behind the computer. On my command. Go."

I followed his orders. I stood up. "I'm over here," I

called out. Two shadows approached, and they rounded the corner. The grey in front raised a vaporizer and I dropped to the floor. Lights burst over my head. *Beeezp! Beeezp! Beeezp!*

I crawled all the way under the desk and hugged my knees to my chest. Had they killed Neptune? Had Neptune killed them? Why was it so quiet? Was everybody dead?

"Get up. You'll want to see this," Neptune said. He held his hand out. Humbled by the events of the day, I accepted his help. He pulled me up and turned me around with his hands on my shoulders. Two grey aliens lay on the ground. Both had numbers marking the back of their hands: 3 and 4. Grey Three's hand was outstretched as if it were reaching for the vaporizer that sat a few feet in front of him. Grey Four held something. It was the weapon Mattix kept in the Dusk Driver in case of emergencies.

Neptune approached the bodies and aimed his gun. He fired. *Beeezp!*

I raced forward to stop him. "Stop! He's already dead!"

"Look at him," Neptune commanded.

I waited for the words "teachable moment," but if that's what Neptune was thinking, he was smart enough to keep it to himself. I looked back at the greys. One was in the same position that I'd found on the floor of the transport deck. Face down, one arm extended.

The other was still alive, and it was crawling our way.

14: SHADES OF GREY

I'd watched two greys come out from engineering and approach. But before that, when I was eavesdropping on them, I heard voices. Real, honest-to-goodness, understandable voices. Did the greys speak English? Or were they talking to someone else on the ship? Was there another victim in engineering—Rune? Was his absence suspicious?

I looked down at the ground and watched the grey reach out to grab Neptune's ankle. I remembered the alien on the transport pad who I thought was dead who wasn't. He'd been in the exact same position. I grabbed Neptune's gun and aimed it at the figure. The grey lifted his oval head and stared at me with giant black eyes.

If Neptune was surprised, he didn't show it. He dropped down and pinned Grey Three to the ground with his knee. He pulled a zip-tie from the pocket of his white captain's uniform. (Did captain uniforms come with zip-ties in their pockets? Should I have known that? What else did he have?) He pulled the restriction tight around the alien's narrow wrists and lifted the captured stowaway to his feet.

I looked at Grey Three and then back at Neptune. "They hear us. They understand us. They talk just like us. I'd rather make my report after you have them secured and we're out of earshot. Of both of them."

"We need an engineer."

"We need a lot of things! But right now, we need to secure these aliens and come up with a plan."

He pushed Grey Three toward me and secured Grey Four. "Put them in the holding cell."

Personal experience taught me about the holding cell, but it turned out the laser barriers used on me were only one of several devices the ship had for the detention of prisoners. Neptune pressed a button on the wall and a panel slid open. I kept one hand on the zip ties on Grey Three and, with the other, grabbed a cord on the end of what turned out to be a hinged, cage-like wall. Neptune followed me and put Grey Four into the holding cell and secured the cord to the opposite wall. Metal rods dropped out of the ceiling and fed through loops in the cage, locking it into place and making it rigid.

The greys weren't going anywhere.

If there was any doubt whether the aliens knew what was happening, their lack of protestation served as proof of their guilt. When Neptune had arrested me, I'd kicked, screamed, and offered up as many possible suspects as I could think of. Silence in a situation like this was as good as a signed confession.

I still wasn't clear on their intended crime.

Neptune and I left security section together. I waited until we were in the elevator with the doors closed before talking. Fast.

"We have a problem. We have like ten problems. Maybe twenty—I lost count. Do you want to go to your quarters to talk?"

"Council Chambers. They're waiting."

"Who's waiting?"

"The crew," Neptune said. "We have to tell them what's going on. We don't have enough crew to run a side operation and keep it from them."

"What are you going to say?"

"Not me. You." The elevator stopped, and the doors opened. I didn't move. "Stryker," Neptune said.

"Me. You want me to lead a meeting in Council Chambers." They were questions—or they should have been. But the ridiculousness of a space academy dropout who'd recently been an accessory to the crime of hijacking a privately-owned ship designed for luxury space travel conducting a meeting in the most private and prestigious room on the ship affected my ability to ask sentences in the properly inquisitive manner.

Neptune leaned down and whispered in my ear. "Yes. We need their help."

I stood a little straighter. Neptune was right. Not counting Doc or T-Fal, there were six crew members on the ship and four of them didn't know what they'd signed up for. Even if we turned back now, we would need everyone to perform double duty to get there. And with Pika in danger on Saturn, I had no intention of turning back now.

I strode down the hall and entered Council Chambers. Like other parts of the mini ship, this room was smaller than the Council Chambers on Moon Units 5 and 6. Sleek white walls and furniture made up the interior. Instead of a station holding individual computer tablets for intel, a single screen was mounted on the wall. It showed our current flight plan.

Our crew was waiting for us: Ivi, Kentaro, Rune, T-Fal, and my dad. Between Ivi's green coloring and my dad's purple shade, Kentaro and Rune stood out by being less definable shades of beige. T-Fal looked freshly polished, his brushed aluminum rice-cooker body and black lid to the pressure cooker that made up his head reflecting the light from the fluorescent tubes overhead. The only crew member who wasn't present was Doc.

"Should we wait for Doc?" I asked Neptune in a low voice.

"He's with the Gremlons." Neptune addressed the crew. "Lieutenant Stryker is acting head of security on this ship. She will brief you on our status." He turned to me.

"Thank you." In the back of my mind, the formal

language required to address the crew in an official setting was buried. But as I scanned the faces of the people in front of me, I knew formal language wasn't what the moment needed. Honesty was. They were entitled to the truth. I looked at Neptune. He pressed his lips together and nodded once. There was no way he could have known what I was thinking, but I took his nod as encouragement.

"This isn't a paid Moon Unit voyage," I said to the crew, "and it isn't a training simulation. We're on a rescue mission. The space pirate Omicron Faarstar murdered a courier and a Federation Council member. We believe a Gremlon witnessed at least one of these crimes and is hiding on Saturn. I don't know much more than that."

"Who hired us?" Ivi asked.

"Each of you responded to a last-minute employment posting. There were no jobs."

"You tricked us into a death mission," she said.

"The witness is Ensign Pika. She was on Moon Unit 6, the trek to Venus. The only intel we have is what she was able to send to us via remote messaging."

I stared directly at Ivi. As a Martian, she would know about what happened on the trip to Venus. And if she answered an ad for a last-minute job to work on Moon Unit Mini 7.2, then she had her reasons for getting away from her kind.

Understanding was present in her eyes. "Forgive me, Lieutenant. I stand ready to serve your mission."

I smiled and nodded, and then looked at the other

two. Rune, whose skills were greener than Ivi's Martian skin. Kentaro, the boyish medic turned purser. T-Fal, who would follow whatever orders were programmed into him. Would they go along with Ivi and join us? Or would they turn us in before we could get to Saturn?

I didn't make eye contact with my dad.

"Who was the courier?" Rune asked.

"Mattix Dusk," I said. "He delivers supplies to the colonies under Federation Council rule."

"I know Mattix," Kentaro said. "He delivered my medical supplies while I was recovering from my injury." He tapped his leg. "I'm in."

That left Rune. His eyes were down, looking at a spot on the floor. If he'd asked to be dropped off at the nearest space station, I would have been relieved. But when he looked up and spoke, it was with a question.

"Do you have any intel to prove your suspicions are accurate? Maybe the transmission Ensign Pika sent you was fake. We could be flying into a trap. Did you think about that?"

I didn't answer, mostly because Rune's question was valid, and I was more interested in why he was the only one asking. While I waited for a reaction from the others, he continued. "You don't know anything about Omicron Faarstar. That dude's evil. He's capable of destroying us because he wants to watch the ship go boom." He held his hands in front of him and shook his head. "I'm sorry. I can't go along with this. Not because you want to save your friend. That's not a good enough reason."

My dad spoke up. "Lieutenant Rune, let me assure you, there is one expert on space pirates on this ship and that expert is me. I've spent over a decade on a Federation Council team that operated with the mission to destroy Cheung Qidd's network. In the wake of his arrest, a new crop of pirates have stepped in and taken over. Faarstar is the most notorious. I've dedicated my life to bringing space pirates to justice. I won't let him keep operational what I swore to destroy."

My dad was an expert on space pirates? He was working on a mission to destroy the man who the galaxy believed had been his partner? And the Federation Council had sanctioned this mission? Rune wasn't the only one with questions anymore. But my questions were too numerous to voice and to do so would have compromised my temporary authority.

My dad's calm reassurance had the proper effect on Rune. The two men shook hands. Rune was on board. We were a stronger unit because we would be operating as one.

The doors to Council Chambers slid open and Doc entered. "What is going on in here?" he demanded.

"Doc," I said. "I thought—we thought—shouldn't you be with the Gremlons?"

"I was until I found out about your little friend here. Have you all lost your minds?"

What was he talking about? The room was

soundproof. How did he know the nature of our discussion?

Before I could develop a cover story or convince Doc we were on the up and up, he pulled a gun out of his holster. "Cooperating with a known criminal is a crime," he said. I watched, horrified, as he pressed the gun to the back of my dad's head and pulled the trigger.

15: WHO'S IN AND WHO'S OUT?

"No!" I screamed. I ran across the room and pulled Doc away from the man who, until this moment, I wasn't sure if I believed in enough to save. But Jack Stryker had just told a room full of strangers that he'd dedicated his life to destroying the man who'd killed his wife. He was our source of intel against the enemy. If we were going to beat a space pirate at anything, we needed someone on the inside and he was the closest thing we had.

I was too late. The gun Doc fired was a chip gun. It injected a subcutaneous chip into the base of a person's skull and could be used to monitor them for the rest of their lives. I saw the injection wound and I saw a trickle of blood, red against his purple skin, drip down his neck and dissolve into the fabric of his shirt.

I grabbed his arm and draped it around my shoulder. His eyes were closed. He leaned on me heavily and it took everything I had not to fall under his weight. Neptune hooked my dad's other arm over his shoulder and lifted the weight off me. "I'll take him to Medi-Bay," he said to Doc.

"Like heck you will," Doc said. "He's a criminal. He belongs in the holding cell. If you aren't going to take him there, then I will."

The men had a stare-off for a few seconds while I questioned what would happen when Doc showed up in security section and discovered two grey aliens already warming the cot.

Rune stepped forward. "Excuse me, Doc? I think you owe the captain a little more respect."

"The captain?" Doc was (understandably) confused. As the meaning of Rune's comment seemed to sink in, Doc's expression went from annoyance to anger. "Somebody made you a captain?" he said to Neptune. He shook his head. "I have to find a new job," he said to himself. He grabbed Jack's arm and pulled him out from under Neptune's hold, and then led him out of the room. Neptune looked at me. I nodded to show I was still with him. He followed Doc and left me with the crew.

When the doors shut, I turned back to the group. Gone were any formalities I'd attempted. It was time to level with them. "What you felt earlier was an attack. Rune's manifests in engineering indicated we were in an asteroid field, so I made the decision to map a new course and go to warp."

"That should have worked," Ivi said. "What was the

problem?"

"The problem was that we weren't flying through space debris or an asteroid field. If we had charted a last-minute course and gone to warp, there would have been no record of where we'd gone or why."

"You made a mistake that could have cost us our lives," Ivi said.

"Based on what Rune told her," Kentaro countered. He turned to his robot. "T-Fal, make a report on the status of the ship."

T-Fal vibrated in a quick wake-up shimmy and then spoke. "Lieutenant Stryker's advice to Captain Neptune was sound. I have run the variables as they happened and would have reached the same conclusion."

Ivi looked from the robot to me. "So why didn't we do it? Doesn't the captain trust your judgment?"

"Something didn't seem right. The view from the bridge showed no flotsam. I checked the exterior cameras on all surfaces on the outside of the ship and realized there was nothing there. If we had charted a new course and gone into warp at that moment, we would have destroyed the ship in flight. Right now, every one of us would be floating in zero gravity waiting to die."

"How could Faarstar have attacked us without you seeing him?"

I turned to T-Fal. I had a hunch how Faarstar had done it but having use of a robot to deliver intel was a convenience I wasn't used to, and I didn't want to waste the opportunity.

"T-Fal, based on the variables you ran, how did Faarstar attack us without us knowing?"

"There is one external location that is not visible from the exterior cameras. Based on the report of damage to the fuel rod and the elimination of threat when Lieutenant Stryker canceled forward thrusters and warp command, my calculations conclude that Faarstar's ship was directly above the Moon Unit Mini 7.2."

Ivi, Kentaro, and Rune all looked up. "Faarstar wanted to goad us into going to warp," Rune said. "He knows we're on our way to Saturn and he's trying to keep us from arriving."

I dropped into a white molded chair and kicked my legs out in front of me. "What we're asking you to do isn't going to be easy, and I understand if you all want to get in the emergency pod and leave. Or if you want to file an official report with Federation Council. We broke rules, and I don't break rules lightly."

"Why did you break them this time?" Ivi asked. Of everybody on the crew, she seemed to be the one who intended to hold me accountable for my decisions, and right then, I knew if I didn't level with her—with them—they wouldn't follow me anywhere.

"Neptune and I have reason to believe there's something bigger going on here than Mattix's murder. Something that involves Omicron Faarstar and grey aliens. We have two in the holding cell—" I glanced at

Rune— "they were in engineering and could have been planning sabotage of our main computer." I slowly looked from face to face to gauge their responses. They were unreadable. I thought about Mattix's lifeless body in his space pod and the desperation of Pika in the message she'd recorded on Cat, and emotions overwhelmed me. "Faarstar took over for Cheung Qidd. He's responsible for destroying my planet. I want justice for Mattix and I care about Pika, but Faarstar needs to be stopped and we're the ones who can do it."

"What are you going to do?" Ivi asked. Despite her short Martian stature, she projected confidence and poise. Her wide yellow eyes were framed with long black lashes which must have been fake since Martians were without body hair.

"You guys don't know anything about me. Let me give you my background in a nutshell. I'm half Plunian and half Earthling. My mom was killed when the space pirates blew up Plunia." I paused for a few seconds before adding, "and my dad was just carted off to a holding cell by Doc Edison."

"Your dad is Jack Stryker?" Rune asked, noticeably surprised. "I heard about him."

Lights inside the smooth black lid on T-Fal's head glowed and rotated. His aluminum base tilted backward and rolled toward the table, and then righted itself. A clicking sound came from inside him, and then his robotic voice spoke: "Jack Stryker. Private businessman. Former owner of Stryker Dry Ice Mines. Arrested for collusion with pirates. Known felon. Under Federation Council Protection. Details are arrest level five classification."

"Yes, my dad is Jack Stryker." I forced myself to take in their faces, so I could internalize the silent judgment that hung in the room. "And yes, Neptune and I stole the Moon Unit Mini 7.2 and made up your assignments to get a crew together to run this mission. When we're done, I'll turn myself in, but I can't do that yet. Not until we stop Faarstar. Pika was with Mattix when he was killed. She's a key witness. We need her to put an end to this."

Ivi walked up to me. With me in the chair, we were the same height. I'd had bad luck with Martians since the first time I'd boarded a Moon Unit and it just figured she was going to be the one to take me down.

She held out her hand. "I'd be proud to be a part of your team. My skill set includes navigation, communication, and basic defense maneuvers."

Ivi wasn't taking me down?

T-Fal rolled past Rune and Kentaro and stopped beside her. "Lieutenant Ivi. Speaks four hundred and six languages. Has experience charting map coordinates on twenty-seven missions. Trained in Muay Thai, Wing Chun, and boxing."

I raised an eyebrow.

She leaned in. "Martian men can be a little rough,"

"So I've heard." I shook her hand and looked up at the other faces.

Kentaro limped forward and stood side by side with Ivi. Despite the youthfulness of his features, there was a world-weary quality about him. I suspected life after his injury hadn't been easy and had taken its toll.

I stood to face him. He looked me straight in the eye and puffed his chest out "I'm in too. I can keep the Gremlons entertained and handle medical. I can program T-Fal to monitor the flight coordinates and diagnostics. And I can work on Doc and see what I can do for your dad."

"Thank you, Kentaro."

T-Fal added: "Medic Kentaro. Of Japanese descent. First trained in space military. Wounded in battle between Mars and Venus. Injury to left leg banned him from future military service. No records for past twenty years."

Kentaro looked embarrassed. "I had a harder time recovering emotionally than physically. Took some time off to get my head together."

I nodded my understanding. I knew what it was like to have emotional scars. "How about you, Rune? What do you say?"

He shook his head. "I don't know what to say. You people aren't anything like what I expected."

Lulled into a false sense of confidence, I now realized it would only take one dissenting crew member to destroy our chances of a successful mission. "What are you going to do?"

"I don't know." He looked at each of us. "I need to think." And the least experienced of all of us walked out, leaving Council Chambers in stunned silence.

16: ONE LESS PERSON TO TRUST

"I can't believe Lieutenant Rune walked out," Ivi said. "Did he not hear you? What you think we're capable of doing or why you want us to try? What did they teach him at Space Academy?"

"Let me worry about Rune," I said. "He's young and inexperienced, and if he doesn't want to help us, we can't make him." I looked at the two volunteers in front of me. I had an idea, but I didn't want to cause any additional alarm. "How well do you two know the layout of the ship?" I asked them.

"There are schematic drawings in the employee cafeteria," Kentaro said. "Why?"

"I'd feel a lot better about what we have to do if I knew you were both suited up properly. Meet me in the uniform ward in ten minutes."

Kentaro and Ivi left. When Council Chambers was down to just me and the robot, I asked him, "T-Fal, report on Rebel Rune."

T-Fal's internal computer clicked several times while his lights rotated through white, blue, yellow, and red. After three rotations, he said what I'd started to suspect. "Error. Rebel Rune does not compute. Error. Rebel Rune does not compute. Error. Rebel—"

I pressed the speech override button and T-Fal stopped mid-sentence. Just as I suspected. On top of everything else, we had a faker on board.

A shot of static filled my ear. "Stryker," Neptune said. "Did I hear T-Fal correctly?"

"Yep."

"Okay. You suit up the crew. Meet me in my quarters when you're done."

"Can't I pick out quarters first?"

"You don't have quarters yet?"

"No. There hasn't been time. I slept in the uniform ward, and my stuff is in security section outside the holding cell."

"No, it's not."

"Yes, it is. I know that's not important in the grand scheme of things, and I know that because I'm part Plunian I don't need a lot of sleep to survive, but still, it would be nice to know I have a cot to call my own."

"Stryker." I stopped talking. "Where did you say you left your gear?"

"In the security hallway between the holding cell and engineering. It's a black backpack, a suitcase with oxygen canisters, and Cat."

"When did you last see it?"

"When you shot the greys. Didn't I tell you? That's how they knew I was there. Somebody shined a flashlight on Cat and he meowed. They came into the hallway to investigate and caught me by the desk."

"We have a problem."

"We have more than one."

"We have a new problem. Your gear is gone. So is Cat. Whoever has him is probably going to find the message Pika sent. We can no longer assume this will be a sneak attack."

***

I met Kentaro and Ivi in the uniform ward. After handing out protein packs and electrolyte drinks, from the supply cabinet (at least the ship was stocked with something to eat), I fitted each of them in yellow, self-fitting Stealthyester® uniforms. In addition to the reflective coating, the latest prototypes had a nearly invisible grid backing the fabric, keeping it cooler, more flexible, and rip resistant. I performed quick alterations with hidden drawstrings on Ivi's, shortening it to Martian measurements. Kentaro was an easier fit because of his slim build, but the injury he'd sustained in battle had left one of his legs slightly longer than the other. I shored the pants up with a cuff secured with reflective tape and added a fresh coating of antibacterial spray since his role as medic might put him closer to potential toxins. When we were finished, I sent both of them on their way and changed into a new uniform myself. In addition to the features on Ivi and Kentaro's, mine had a hidden pouch for my oxygen tank and a tunnel for the lens of a body camera. I slipped the camera into place and tested it before setting it to sleep mode and leaving.

Neptune expected me in his quarters, but I had another stop to make first. One that would take as much energy as I could summon to survive.

I balled my old uniform up and tossed it in the laundry bin and then sealed the ward and went to Ion-54. It was the after-hours club on all Moon Units and was outfitted with shiny mirrored walls and a glowing floor of colorful light-up squares. It was intended to be the party spot for couples who wanted to dance the night away on the ship. And even though we had no entertainment director or purser on board, it was where I expected to find the forty-seven Gremlons.

My suspicions were spot-on.

I heard the music before I reached the door. A pulsing dance beat spilled into the hallway, and I found myself walking in time with it. The door was open. I slipped inside and stared at the crowd of soft, pink aliens. To my right, a Gremlon was on the shoulders of another Gremlon on the shoulders of a third Gremlon. The top one was within inches of touching the reflective silver orb that dangled over the colorful dance floor.

Other Gremlons chirped at each other, repeating words and phrases while bouncing from one side of the room to the other. Cross breezes from two separate fans pushed the glittering silver orb to sway and spin, and light bounced off the thousands of mirrored squares on the surface. A few Gremlons chased after the reflected light, trying to grab it in in their large, flat hands. Others sat in a circle underneath it, staring up as if hypnotized.

The reflected light landed on my reflective uniform, and since one of these things was not like the other, I soon became the center of attention. Gremlons approached me with eyes trained on my body. One reached out and touched my boob! I jumped and turned away. The sudden movement scared them, and they stepped back, collectively, with fear in their eyes.

"Shhhh, it's okay," I said. "I'm Sylvia. I'm your friend."

"friend friend friend," said one, while another said, "sparkle sparkle sparkle." Other words were spoken but blended together. The skinny pink aliens formed a circle around me. The stack of Gremlons who had almost reached the silver orb dismantled as first one, then the other nimbly climbed down the one underneath him. If I didn't already have first-hand experience with the peaceful, playful nature of Gremlons through Pika, I might have feared for my safety.

"I'm one of the crew members on the ship," I said. "We're going to Saturn. You know that, right?"

"Contest! Contest! Contest!"

"Won! Won! Won!"

"That's right." Did they understand that only five of them were supposed to be on the ship? That didn't matter so much now. They were here, and I needed their cooperation. Pika's life might depend on it.

The lives of the forty-seven Gremlons facing me depended on it too.

With sickening clarity, I realized my fake contest had the potential to wipe out the lives of the entire group in the room with me. They weren't trained to fight. They weren't trained to defend themselves. When scared, they shrank by about 35 percent, and if that didn't make them appear vulnerable enough, to curl into balls that attackers could kick about. I'd watched Pika get into trouble simply because she was trusting. I had to keep the Gremlons locked up where they were safe. Telling them the truth would only endanger them.

I forced a smile to my face. "As a member of the Moon Unit Mini 7.2 crew, I wanted to welcome you and invite you to stay in Ion-54 as long as you want. I'll bring you Plunian ice cream, and the lights and the mirror orb will twinkle the whole time you're here."

A little pink Gremlon, half as tall as the others, separated from the crowd and stepped up to me. "Miss Purple Lady? When do we get to see Pika?"

I bent down closer and she stepped back and hid behind another Gremlon's legs. I dropped down to a squat so my eyes were at her level. I used a somewhat cheap ploy of angling my shoulders back and forth so the fabric of my uniform caught the light. The little Gremlon's eyes widened. She came back out and reached her hand out to touch me.

"How do you know Pika?" I asked.

"She's one of us," she said. "She told us we could trust you."

"When?"

"When she was in the cat."

"Is she still in the cat?"

The little Gremlon's eyes widened but she didn't reply.

I changed the question. "Do you know where Pika is now?"

She pointed behind her at the crowd.

I looked up at the other Gremlon faces. The fear was gone and in its place was excitement. They knew something I didn't, and they wanted to tell me. "Who knows where Pika is? Can you raise your hand?"

I held my hand up to show them what I meant. One by one, skinny pink arms went up in the air. That wasn't possible. How could all forty-seven of them—or as many of them that I could see while they were crowded together like that—know where Pika was?

"Can one of you tell me?"

The group huddled closer together. I stood and picked a canister of colorful sugar crystals from one of the tables. I unscrewed the top and ran my hand through it, and then threw it in the air like confetti.

It had the desired effect. The Gremlons scattered around the room trying to catch the crystals. If I'd thought to switch off the gravity in the room it would have been even more effective (although corralling forty-seven floating Gremlons would have been a separate challenge). When the crowd had dispersed enough, a single Gremlon was left standing at the back, alone, holding the one thing that explained how they knew what they knew.

My robot, Cat. The Gremlons learned about Pika the same way I had. Which meant they already knew she was in trouble.

17: INNOCENCE LOST

"Hi," I said, as I approached the Gremlon. "I'm Sylvia."

The small pink character in front of me was a boy. The easiest way to tell the difference between male and female Gremlons was their build. Females were tall and skinny, built like the stick inside an oxygen pop. Males were short and plump, like the spoons used to eat Plunian ice. It was an easy distinction.

"I'm Yoka," he said.

"Cat is friendly, isn't he? Did he behave himself?"

"Is he yours?"

I nodded. "Did you take my other things? The suitcase and backpack outside of security section?"

Yoka looked scared. "I didn't take the cat," he said. "I didn't take anything."

Yoka set Cat on the ground. Cat didn't move. I normally only used Cat's recognition of audible commands in the privacy of my room, but right now, there was a benefit to displaying what Cat could do. Invoking trust.

"Cat, wake up."

Cat's eyes lit, and he shifted from side to side. He meowed.

"Cat, walk," I said.

Cat's white fiberglass legs moved stiffly but carried him one small step at a time while the Gremlons *ooohed* and *aaaahed* as expected. I addressed Yoka, knowing the other Gremlons were listening. "Cat knows me. He told me about Pika already. She's in trouble and I'm trying to help her."

Yoka stood still. The little girl who had asked me about Cat earlier ran up to him and dropped down on all fours. She touched her nose to his head. "Show me Pika," she said.

Cat's eyes turned off and he stopped walking.

What they didn't know was that I'd modified more of Cat than I'd left untouched. In addition to the data recorder, the microchip, the internal projector, the hidden storage compartments, and the alarm clock, he was programmed to recognize one voice. I'd considered adding Neptune but couldn't picture him giving commands to a robot cat. I'd considered adding Pika but couldn't imagine what she'd ask Cat to do. My indecision had left things the way they'd been: with Cat responding to only one voice: mine.

The girl looked at me. "Did I kill him?"

"Of course not!" I said quickly. "Cat, wake up." Cat's

eyes glowed and he rocked from side to side. The girl clapped.

I focused my attention on the girl. "You told me Pika was inside the cat but isn't anymore, and you said you knew where she went."

"No. I knew where Cat went."

"Where did Cat go?"

"With Yoka."

"Do you know what Yoka did with Pika?"

"Pika was gone before Yoka took Cat."

That didn't make sense. "You mean you saw the projection of Pika, and then later when Yoka had Cat, you couldn't get the projection of Pika to work?"

She shook her head. "Pika was inside the cat and now Pika isn't inside the cat."

I had my work cut out for me.

I wasn't the only one who thought so. "Styrker."

"Neptune."

The Gremlon's eyes widened and she got smaller. She backed away from me and hid behind the other Gremlon legs. I'd forgotten that nobody else could hear the voice in my head, and suddenly speaking in a different tone, in response to someone who wasn't there, had startled her.

"Check the disc drive in your cat," he said.

I picked Cat up and flipped him over. The data chip was missing. Which made sense. The Gremlons had found Cat somewhere. I already knew their prying fingers could find buttons and switches and compartments that no other person would think to discover. Five minutes of exploring and their fingers would have had the image of Pika playing on a nearby wall. But who had stolen the disc? Had one of them taken it accidentally or was someone on the ship wise to the intel Pika had sent us? Why hadn't I forced Neptune to sit down and watch what I'd watched and examined every byte of data on Cat to make sure Pika hadn't recorded anything else?

Because Gremlons weren't expected to do things like that. They weren't wired to record suspicious behavior or distrust those around them. They were playful. They could make people laugh. They were natural born entertainers. They were soft and cuddly and funny and sweet and goofy and innocent.

Something had changed that in Pika. She knew to record the message that led us on this mission. She recognized the threat of space pirates and the need to ask for help from Neptune and me. It had nothing to do with her being a Gremlon and everything to do with her spending time with us. We'd changed her. The exposure to bad guys on the two previous Moon Units had taught her that everybody wasn't her friend.

In a way, that thought saddened me. But while it was inevitable that Pika learned those lessons if she were to survive on her own, there was a different Gremlon who seemed to have learned the same lesson. One who hadn't been on the previous moon treks, hadn't spent time around Neptune, and by all apparent measures seemed to have the protection of her race.

Did I kill him? the little Gremlon had asked.

How did a Gremlon understand the concept of killing?

18: BACKGROUND CHECK

"The drive is empty," I said out loud. "Someone has the disc." The Gremlons watched me talk, apparently still confused by who I was talking to.

"You watched the projection since we departed?" Neptune asked.

"Yes."

"Then someone on the ship knows what we know."

"Yes."

"Trust no one."

"Except you," I said.

There was a beat of silence. "Yes. Trust me."

I stood up and tucked Cat under my arm. He felt cold next to my warm Plunian skin. The air in Ion-54, like all the passenger-facing parts of the ship, was a half and half mix of oxygen and nitrogen. It wasn't just the relative comfort of being surrounded by the sweet Gremlons that made me feel better. It was the air quality. Unlike the thin air in security section, up here, I was at the top of my game.

Despite that, I left. The longer I stayed with the Gremlons, the more I'd want to stay with the Gremlons. That was part of their charm. They could easily distract you into losing hours of time with their inherent silliness. It seemed I'd learned something from Pika as well.

At this rate, there wasn't much point in picking a room. My belongings were gone from where I'd left them. I should have been happy the Gremlons had Cat. He was the only thing I had left. I followed the corridor to the captain's quarters and waved my hand in front of the sensor.

Nothing happened. I pressed my hand in front of the sensor while a beam of light scanned the palm of my hand. A red light rejected the print. Finally, I balled up my fist and knocked.

The doors swished open and Neptune stood in front of me. "Stryker."

"Captain," I said.

"Call me Neptune."

"Don't you think the crew will think that's weird? You are the acting captain. So *act* like the *captain*."

"When we're alone in my room, call me Neptune."

I pushed past him and entered. "You have a real problem being the captain, don't you? What's that about?" He didn't answer. "Fine. Neptune, we have a problem."

"A new one?"

"The Gremlons understand the concept of killing. I think it's because they watched the disc. But now the disc is gone and with it goes our intel."

"Not completely."

I sensed Neptune had been holding out on me, and it turned out I was right. He pressed his palm onto the computer identification pad and stood still while a green beam of light scanned his eye. When his identity was confirmed, he typed in a series of commands and a file appeared on the screen. He pressed the play button and the image of Pika appeared.

"Now you be a good cat, okay? Go get Sylvia and tell her we need her help. But don't tell the giant. If he finds out I went to Saturn, he'll be mad mad mad. I know Sylvia kept my secret. She promised. Bye-bye, Cat."

"That was on the data chip," I said. "How did you copy the data chip? Those files have a built-in corruption code. If someone tries to copy them, they activate the data scrambler and the information wipes itself out. I know. I built it."

"How would you do it?"

"Oh, come on! This is real danger here. I think we're beyond the lesson plan."

He glared at me, and I got mad. "I don't know how I'd do it because in the real world, I would ask the person I'm supposed to be able to trust and he'd tell me how he did it. But you can't do that, can you? You want me to trust you, but you don't trust me."

"Stryker—"

"I'm tired of your lessons and your secrets and your

top-secret intel about my family that I'm not allowed to know. You know what this is? It's fake." I waved my hands around the room. "I don't know what you know. I don't know why everybody said my dad was in jail but now I find out he wasn't. I don't know why I lived most of my life believing I was raised by a criminal. But you do. All this 'we're in this together' and 'I'll look out for you' is phony. I need something real, Neptune. Stop trying to make me figure everything out and tell me something I don't know."

His voice softened. "I want to tell you the truth, but the truth can get you killed. Before I'm willing to take that chance, I need to know that I've taught you what you need to save yourself."

This was what I wanted, right? I wanted to learn. I wanted a mentor. I wanted the knowledge that I would have gotten from my education if my life had gone a different direction. What Neptune offered me was the closest I'd ever come to getting it.

I looked up at him. "I know how Cat works and I know you can't copy his files. The only way you could have that intel is if you have the original disc."

He raised one eyebrow. "I don't have the original disc."

"Then you didn't replay the message."

"No, I didn't."

"You—you—you recorded the recording?" I sputtered. "When I first projected it on the side of Mattix's ship? When it landed on the helipad?" He nodded. That was genius. It was so low-tech, nobody would have thought to do that. "How did you know we'd need it?"

"When you acquire a valuable piece of intel, you find a way to protect it. Pika loves Cat and she knew her only chance at survival was to record that message and send Cat to tell you. She may not understand that Cat isn't a real cat, but she's watched you interact with him enough to know you treat him like he's real."

Neptune was right. I treated Cat like a companion, not like a toy. Not around him, but around Pika, I did. It was because she brought out my playful side and didn't judge me. Around Neptune I tried to act strong. I had no idea he'd seen me act that way around Cat and knowing he had was humbling. Maybe it was time to drop the act and let Neptune know what I was hiding under the surface of the back talk and attitude.

I sat on the corner of Neptune's bed. "When my dad was arrested, people treated me like a pariah. They assumed my mom and I were in on the partnership with the space pirates. Like a get-rich-quick scheme. You already know I dropped out of the academy, but what you don't know is that a couple of things happened before it got to that point."

Neptune stood in front of me. He reached his hand out and took mine. "I know about your background."

"You don't know this."

Neptune and I both had skeletons in our closets, but neither one of us was a victim. It was time to take responsibility for what had led to my expulsion from school. The truth. Not the story I'd repeated since it happened.

Neptune sat on the bed next to me. I stared ahead, not wanting to see the look on his face when I confessed.

"I got into schoolyard fights," I said. "Verbal. And then physical. I acted out. At first, it was only after being baited, but it got to the point where instead of being on the defense, I went on the offense. I sent four students home with injuries after starting a fight outside the language lab. Three humans and a Martian." I paused before sharing the worst. "The Martian never recovered." I'd been staring at my hands, clenched together in front of me, because it pained me to talk about those days. I forced myself to look at Neptune. "When I realized what I'd done, I turned myself in to the dean. It was grounds for expulsion. But in light of my father's arrest, the dean agreed to keep the details confidential. To the rest of the world, I dropped out to go back to Plunia to work with my mom, but somewhere there's a sealed file that says what really happened."

"You've had a history with Martian confrontation," he said.

"There's a chance I had something to do with their hatred of Plunians."

"Why are you telling me this?"

"You said I could trust you."

"Is that the only reason?"

"No." I stood up and faced him. "For us to realistically consider all the potential problems on this trip, you needed to know the truth. My truth. And it's relative to our situation because there's a Martian on this ship and I'm not sure we should count her out from the suspect list."

19: RECAPPING THE SUSPECTS

I didn't expect Neptune to tell me everything was going to be okay or to be impressed with my confession. I told him for the sake of telling him. If we were going to operate as a team, he needed to know the details about my background: the good, the bad, and the ugly.

He stood. "After talking to the Gremlons, what's your report?"

"I don't know," I said honestly. "They saw Pika's projection coming from Cat, so they know she's in trouble. But if someone else has the disc, someone else knows too. Or not."

"Explain."

"It's entirely possible that someone on this ship knows what we're up to. I'm not sure I trust Rune—he's never been on a Moon Unit before and his references could have been faked. He could have shown up to keep an eye on us or to run interference and keep us from getting to Saturn. As the engineer, he's capable of completely throwing us off course."

"Who else?"

"We already know there are greys on board. We caught two but Grey Two is still MIA. Were the greys here all along? Or did they come on with the Gremlons? Do they have anything to do with Grey One from the helipad? Or are they slowly spreading throughout the galaxy and them showing up was random?"

"Next."

"Doc. Why did he show up? He's smart enough to know the scheduler didn't make a mistake. And even if he thought that was true, don't you think he would have checked it out? He's a doctor, not a spaceman. He doesn't particularly like you. And even though he's been nice enough to me in the past, he's very by the book. He chipped my dad without a second thought."

"Doc being here presents problems but not the problems you think."

"What does that mean?"

"Keep going with your suspects."

"T-Fal."

"Kentaro's robot?"

"Yes. What do we know about him? He's a robot so he's programmed to take orders, but he's programmed to take *Kentaro's* orders. Just like I programmed Cat to take mine. What if Kentaro wired T-Fal for personal use?"

"What did Kentaro's background check say?"

"He's a medic. Military trained. Sustained injuries in a battle between Mars and Venus and was honorably discharged."

Neptune didn't like that. "Where'd you get that intel?"

"T-Fal," I said.

"The battle between Mars and Venus was two decades ago. Where's he been since?"

"No records for the past twenty years. He said he dropped off the grid. Or it could mean he didn't think it was necessary to program his history into his robot."

"If it's public knowledge, T-Fal would get it through the information database."

"Okay, so Kentaro dropped out of society. That happens, right? When someone stops interacting with the public, the system stops recording their behavior. No records could mean nothing." *Like you,* I wanted to add, but I didn't.

"And then there's the Gremlons," I said before getting off track.

"What about the Gremlons?" Neptune asked. "Gremlons aren't violent."

"I know. And I think if Gremlons had anything to do with Pika, we would have gotten an entirely different recording from the disc. But Gremlons found Cat on the ship and figured out how to run his projector. One of them could have knocked the disc out of Cat when they were playing with him, or pocketed the disc and forgotten about it, or thought it was a snack and eaten it, or hidden it in something shiny."

"That's possible?"

"Have you never seen how wily Pika is when it comes to hiding stuff she doesn't want you to find?"

"Like what?"

"Like your dog tags. I found them sewn into the lining of my thermal sleepwear. You didn't even know they were missing."

Something flashed across Neptune's face. An expression I wasn't used to seeing. It was there and then gone, so quickly that I wondered if I'd imagined it. That story meant something to him and I was left in the dark.

"Keep an eye on the Gremlons." He stared at me intensely. "You left out one suspect."

"I know."

"Where do you stand on him?"

My dad. In a holding cell on the floor underneath us with the greys. Chipped by Doc. Jack Stryker had been arrested, tried, and convicted. He'd spent the better part of my life in prison. And all that time, he'd managed to avoid being shot with the very tracking chip that a Moon Unit doctor had injected after less than a day on board a stolen cruise ship.

"I don't know," I said. "He's a stranger to me."

Neptune lowered himself to the bed next to me. We faced the same direction, staring at the wall in front of us, with our thighs barely touching. When Neptune spoke, it wasn't what I expected.

"Jack Stryker was recruited to work with a secret branch of the Federation Council to infiltrate and destroy the space pirate network. He posed as a dry ice miner and when Cheung Qidd approached him, Jack followed orders to play along. He collected valuable intel that led to the arrest and incarceration of the most notorious pirate in the galaxy. If people knew what he did, he'd be a hero."

"People don't treat me like I'm the daughter of a hero."

"The mission wasn't without risks and one of those risks was the possibility of never seeing you or your mother again. He agreed because he knew a galaxy without space pirates would be safer for both of you. But you were his weakness. Qidd found out about you and used you to punish Jack."

"And my mom?"

"Federation Council wasn't prepared for Qidd to relinquish control of his army to Faarstar. When Qidd asked for counsel and told FC about the extent of his network, Faarstar blew up Plunia. He declared war, not only against your father, but against Qidd. Faarstar's move was a proclamation of his power. He destroyed a planet to say he was more powerful than Qidd ever was."

"Why didn't you tell me?

"I have questions about how Federation Council handled your dad's arrest. Until I have answers, anything I say would jeopardize your safety."

"And now my dad is here on the ship. I don't know how he got out of prison. I don't know if he's being hunted. I don't know if he's part of a trap."

I searched Neptune's face for a sign that we could do this without relying on my dad, a sign that Neptune had a plan that a former military officer and a space academy dropout could handle on their own.

"Stryker, I was on the team that brought your father in to Federation Council. I thought you should know."

"You were there? On Plunia?"

"No. I was waiting on Colony 13."

I remembered that day. It was the day I stopped dreaming of a future in Federation Council security and started taking care of myself.

Neptune continued. "We were told he was a traitor. I believed that until I met you. I started asking questions that people didn't want to answer. I suspect there's real corruption in the FC and your dad is caught in the middle."

"You were supposed to teach at the academy and you lost your credentials. Right after I was expelled. Is that timing suspicious?"

"Somebody thought it would be a bad idea for you and me to meet," he said. "I've figured out that much. I just haven't figured out who."

20: SLEEPING ARRANGEMENTS

It was too much information to process. Was my dad good or bad? Had he been working for the Federation Council or had he turned to Qidd's side while on the mission? Had he done what had been asked of him and someone on the Federation Council set him up to take the fall for their involvement with Qidd's network?

And why had Qidd broken the pirate code? Had he known Faarstar would destroy Plunia? Was that his goal or was this a power struggle between pirate networks?

The only thing I knew, deep down, was that Neptune was right. I had to come to terms with my dad's presence on the ship sooner rather than later. Until this mission was complete, I had to pick a side: he's my dad or he's the enemy. There was no way I could accept him as both.

My silence must have communicated as much to Neptune. He stood and opened the closet by the front of his room. A suspiciously familiar backpack and suitcase that I strongly suspected contained canisters of oxygen and bundles of freeze-dried ice cream were inside.

"What are my things doing in your closet? Where did you get them?"

"I found them in the hallway outside engineering. Whoever took them put them back. You said you hadn't picked out quarters yet. You're staying here."

"No, I'm not."

"Yes, you are." He crossed his arms and stood with his feet shoulder-width apart. "You are being watched. You said yourself you don't know who to trust. We can talk in here without the threat of being overheard. This room is next to the bridge. Do you want me to continue?"

"Where do you expect me to sleep? You only have one bed." As soon as the words were out of my mouth, I felt myself flush. I tried—unsuccessfully—to think of things like Plunian ice cream and space pirates and computer hacking—things that would take away the energetic vibrations I felt around Neptune. I turned my head slightly and caught my reflection in the mirror over his bar. Yep, my skin was aglow.

I turned back, crossed my arms, stood with my feet shoulder-width apart, and tried to raise one eyebrow. I probably failed, but at least it broke the tension.

"You're going to sleep in the bed. I'll sleep elsewhere."

"How's that going to look to the crew?"

"Which part?"

"Either. Both. If anybody sees you sleeping outside the captain's quarters, they're going to suspect something. If anybody sees me sleeping here, they're going to suspect something entirely different. We can't afford crew gossip right now."

"We can't afford to get distracted by something as minor as rooming arrangements."

"That's my point!"

"Stryker."

He took two steps toward me and grabbed my forearm. Instinct took over. I softened my knees and flipped his hand off me and then grabbed his wrist with my opposite hand and, keeping the momentum going, pushed it down past my torso.

Neptune was caught off guard. His shoulder followed his arm, putting his face near my knee. If this were a fight to the finish, I could slam my knee upward and into his nose. Maybe break it. It was a testament to how much I trusted him that I released him before doing any real damage. I kept my knees slightly bent and my arms raised, a classic fighter's stance, because that was what I'd been taught to do.

Neptune rolled his shoulder backward as if to loosen it up. He kept his eyes on me. He put one hand on his joint and massaged the skin.

"It was instinct," I said. "You grabbed me and I rea—"

I didn't get to finish my sentence. Neptune interrupted me with a sweeping kick that sent me crashing to the ground.

Game on.

I did a backward somersault and pushed myself up to a standing position. My gravity boots gave me additional stability. I'd managed to put distance between us, but Neptune was bigger, stronger, and tougher than I was. He could probably leap across the room and tackle me from where he stood. And he looked ready to pounce. His center of gravity was low, his knees bent. He was trying to figure out my next move just like I was trying to figure out his. Sure, I could charge him. We could tussle like Mattix and I had when he trained me. I was pretty sure Neptune wouldn't hurt me but was it worth the effort? Training was one thing. Wasting time fighting in his room was another. And as confident as I was in my fighting abilities, I was no dummy. We had bigger issues.

Neptune charged. I swung my hand behind me and slapped the gravity pulse deactivation button. I ducked out of the way and watched Neptune rise through the air toward the ceiling. He threw a punch, knowing full well I was out of range. I smiled. "Mattix taught me all sorts of tricks in our fight lessons. Fight smart, not hard. Use your surroundings. See your opponent's differences as weaknesses. Exploit them."

"Differences?"

"You're barefoot and I'm in gravity boots."

He crossed his arms while floating above me. "Good job, Stryker. Mattix taught you well."

I would have normally glowed under the unexpected praise, but something distracted me. Something about Mattix, our lessons, and what he'd taught me when we trained. My mind spun through pieces of information, memories, and fractured images before I realized something crucial.

"We have to watch the video again," I said. "There's another message in there."

"This fight isn't over."

I glanced across the room at the computer. If the door hadn't opened from my hand, then the computer wouldn't activate either. Neptune was the only one who could retrieve the data.

I shook my head. "Fine, you win." I slapped my hand on the gravity button and Neptune crashed to the floor.

21: MR. ROBOTO

I extended my hand to help him up. "Truce?"

Neptune ignored my hand and stood on his own. "What did you remember?"

"Mattix. He had to have been alive when Pika recorded that message. He had to have been alive when the space pod took off. Pika doesn't know how to fly a space pod. She's inquisitive and her fingers like to explore things, but there's no way she could figure out how to take off, map coordinates to your place, turn on the autopilot, record a message on Cat, and activate the buffer zones—all before leaving Saturn. It's just not possible. You know this. I know this."

"What do you think happened?"

"Mattix was alive when they left. Maybe programmed the buffers because he knew he was going to die. Maybe he did everything he did to protect Pika and get the message to us."

Neptune moved to the computer and pressed his hand against the touchpad. A beam of light recorded his palmprint and then unlocked the system. A separate beam shot out and scanned his right eye.

"Welcome, Captain," a female computer voice said.

Neptune's fingers moved quickly over the keys. I'd watched him work at a computer before and knew he was fast and efficient at accessing files. It was a way of life with him. Brevity. Conservation of speech, movement, action.

"Watch," he said.

This was the fourth time I watched the video. I had already memorized what Pika said. This time I focused on other things. Pika set Cat down and talked to him, but Mattix's space pod was behind her. The image was grainy, being a recording of a recording, but I was able to make out letters on the side of the ship.

"Pause it," I said. "There." I pointed to the screen. "That's the Dusk Driver. Pika's leaning against the ship. And look. It's vibrating. The dust underneath it is swirling. The ship was already ready to go."

"What else do you notice?"

"Come on, Neptune, this isn't an exercise. It's real, and this is all we have to go on."

"What else do you notice?" he repeated.

There was no point arguing. I tuned out Neptune, the blinking light on the computer, the previous tension in the room, everything, and focused on the short video clip of Pika. I looked past her into the ship. I saw movement off screen. What was that?

"Go back."

The video rewound a few frames and then played. "Slow it down." Neptune slowed down the images until he was moving frame by frame. And that's when I saw something I'd missed on all the previous viewings.

"Pause," I said. The image froze. I stood up and approached the wall. Off to the side of the screen, barely visible through the open door, was an arm. And the arm was connected to an aluminum body that had been made up from various parts of non-stick cookware and kitchen appliances.

"Zoom," Neptune said.

The image magnified, growing larger on the wall. It became blurry and hard to pick out the objects in the frame. "That's T-Fal," he said.

"Yes. He was on Saturn when Pika and Mattix were sent back to us." I looked away from the screen at Neptune. "Someone could have sent him to the Dusk Driver to program it. It would have been safe and easy. He's a robot. He was following orders, and he's programmed to activate panels and shields and map coordinates and anything else he needed to do to get that ship back to us."

"You think the robot is behind this?"

"No, but the person who programmed the robot could be."

"Kentaro."

I nodded. "But before we say or do anything, we need to find a way to isolate T-Fal."

Neptune stared at me and I felt less like I was being scrutinized and more like we were communicating silently. If his teachable moments had been evidence that he already knew whatever it was that he wanted me to figure out, then he might already have figured this out too.

"You think Pika programmed a message into T-Fal too?" he asked.

"It makes sense, doesn't it? She would have thought he was her friend like Cat."

"Come on. We don't have a lot of time." He headed for the door.

I ran after him and grabbed his arm. His forward momentum wasn't affected in the least. I planted the soles of my gravity boots on the inside wall and used all of my muscle power to keep him from leaving the room.

"What?" he asked.

I walked my feet down the wall until I was standing again. "Where are we going?"

"To security section. Kentaro programmed T-Fal to monitor the greys."

A feeling of alarm washed over me. I pushed Neptune out of the way and took off for the stairs. My boots thundered on the metal as I pounded down them and the sound echoed in the narrow hallway. I burst through the door and ran past engineering to the holding cell.

By the time Neptune caught up to me, I was kneeling

next to my dad's body. He was unconscious with a puddle of blood pooling under his head. The security barrier had been deactivated, and Grey Three and Four were gone.

22: NEXT VICTIM

Neptune grabbed my arm and pulled me up. "It could be a trap," he said.

I shook off his grip. "He needs help."

"Call Doc."

"Kentaro could be in Medi-Bay."

"Call Doc." Neptune unsheathed his space gun. "I'm going to the bridge."

I understood. As bad as the scene down here was, if there were loose greys on the ship, then who knew what they wanted. Divide and conquer. It was our only chance to get ahead of whoever wanted to keep us from arriving at Saturn.

I radioed Medi-Bay. "Security section to Medi-Bay. Code Navy Blue. Repeat, Code Navy Blue."

"Who is this. Sylvia? Don't challenge me on this. I know he's your dad but he's an escaped convict. I've already contacted Federation Council and arranged for them to meet us on Saturn."

"Doc!" I said sharply. "There was a breach. My dad—the prisoner—needs medical help."

"But—"

"Now, Doc. Confidential. Come to security section. Please hurry."

"I'll be right there."

I knew Neptune was right. We didn't know what had happened. We—I—hadn't even admitted if I was ready to trust my dad. He could be faking, or collaborating with the greys, or booby-trapped, or positioned to release a toxic gas in security, or ready to attack—

"Sylvia," he said. His eyes opened and closed, opened and closed. "Is that you?"

"Dad," I said. Everything I'd just thought melted away. I dropped back down on my knees and sandwiched his hand between mine. "Doc's on his way. Hang on. He'll fix you."

"It's not what you think," he said.

"Shhh. We'll have time to talk when you're better. Relax." What was taking Doc so long? My dad coughed. I recognized the sound. He was struggling to get breathable air. I pulled a sublingual oxygen tablet out of my pocket and slipped it into his mouth. He closed his eyes and the tablet dissolved. He was all Plunian, not half like me, and it would be harder for his system to equalize in the thin air down here. The oxygen tablet would help.

The elevator arrived, and Doc stepped out. I held my

breath until I knew he was alone. "Stand back. I need room," he said.

I eased myself away from my dad's body and stood. "He's low on oxygen. I gave him a tablet. He's drifting in and out. Neptune and I found him bleeding on the floor of the cell."

Doc held his infrared thermometer an inch from my dad's temple. The device beeped. Doc's face twisted into concern when he checked the reading.

"I need this area quarantined," he said.

"Why? What—what's wrong?"

"This man is extremely sick. I can't move him. Tell that security ape masquerading as the captain that his holding cell is off limits. I'm using it to operate. Get Kentaro."

"No," I said.

"That wasn't a question, Lieutenant, and the last time I checked, your rank was below mine. Now get Kentaro and tell him to bring that robot of his. I'm going to need help."

I stood with my feet rooted to the floor and not because the magnetic paint was interacting with the soles of my gravity boots. Doc had issued a command and I had to follow it. But that command was a death knell for my dad.

"Stryker," Neptune's voice barked in my ear. "Follow orders."

"Doc—"

"Now."

I ran out of security section and up to the main corridor of the ship.

To say I was conflicted was an understatement. Following orders could lead to my dad's death. Was this it? Was this how I determined what he meant to me? If he was guilty, was it more important for me to have him—my only living relative—in my life and shut out the world like I had when he was first taken away, or to turn off any emotions I had for him and turn him over to the people I now suspected of being behind Mattix's murder?

I was more twisted than the tentacles of a space squid.

I arrived in Medi-Bay and found Kentaro kneeling to the side of T-Fal with a screwdriver. "Hey, Sylvia," Kentaro said. "You okay?"

"Doc needs you in security section. There's an injured passenger who requires emergency surgery."

Kentaro's eyes widened. He stood slowly and dropped the screwdriver. It landed on the carpet with a thud. "Did he say what equipment he needed?"

"He has his emergency kit." I cataloged Kentaro's responses. Nerves: check. Anxiety: check. Shiftiness: check. Despite his age, somewhere in his forties, Kentaro's youthful expression, coupled with his noticeable fear, left him looking like a scared child. The news had left him shaken, and for a medic, the news of an emergency surgery should have triggered a second-nature response.

He turned his back on me and removed a large, blue plastic case from the medical cabinet, opened it and scanned the contents, and slammed it shut.

"He wants T-Fal too," I said.

"No," Kentaro said. The nervousness was back. "He malfunctioned, and I haven't had a chance to figure out where the problem is. He's non-operational."

I looked at the robot. And at Kentaro. And at the robot. "How long have you been working on him?"

"I found him outside Ion-54 two hours ago. His eyes were on the blink and his access panel was missing. If the Gremlons were messing around with him, he probably short-circuited, but I need time to figure out where."

"Stryker," Neptune said in my ear.

"Kentaro, Doc is waiting for you. Leave T-Fal here. I'll seal Medi-Bay per the BOP. There's no time to waste."

Kentaro carried the blue plastic case to the door. I palmed the screwdriver when his back was turned. I left Medi-Bay with him and waited after the elevator doors closed behind him and the indicator panel dinged that the elevator had arrived in security section before going back to fry the door open circuits by jamming them with the screwdriver.

"Stryker," Neptune said again. "Don't sabotage the circuit boards. The door is coded for your palmprint."

I pressed my hand on the touchpad and the doors opened. "Are you watching me?" I asked.

"I prefer to think of it as monitoring my crew. Do you

copy?"

"Loud and clear. Stryker out."

I flipped the operating lights on and accessed T-Fal's data panel. If there was one thing I knew how to do, it was disassemble and reassemble an electronic device. If I was right that T-Fal was present when Pika sent her message to me, then T-Fal's attack made him as much of a victim as my dad.

23: RASPBERRY PI

While Doc and Kentaro started the not-small task of saving my dad's life in the temporary operating room of security section, I performed an operation of my own on T-Fal's circuit board.

It was the single thing I could have done to take my mind off everything. I'd long ago learned to fix, tweak and build things. I wrote and programmed code in homemade computers, repaired appliances for families on Plunia who otherwise would have had nothing to do with me, and retrofitted equipment to ease the burden on the workers in our dry ice mines. It was how I'd first met Mattix. The Dusk Driver had needed repairs and I'd done them in exchange for lodging and free fighting lessons. Now Mattix was dead, the Dusk Driver was compromised, and I'd committed a space felony by hijacking a Moon Unit to try to save a Gremlon who might not live to see her next birthday.

Yes, having a circuit board to focus on was a very good thing.

I twisted a wire here, bent a ribbon cable there, and double checked all the existing connections. I found the problem twenty-three minutes into the process.

A small copper penny from Earth was sandwiched between two magnetic endpoints, interrupting the flow of current. I slipped the penny out, connected the endpoints, and switched on T-Fal's power.

"T-Fal at your service. State your name for recognition."

"Lieutenant Sylvia Stryker."

"Sylvia Stryker. Space Cadet at Academy. Left before graduation. Half Plunian. Respiratory challenged. Recently employed with Moon Unit Corporation."

"Yes, that's me." I stood back and stared at the robot. Did he understand verbal commands? "T-Fal, request playback of last recorded message."

"Message pending," he said. "Download or play?"

"Play." I whirled him to face the cabinet—the best I could do for a blank surface—and held my breath. Remembering how Neptune had made a recording of Pika's recording on Cat, I switched on the body cam that was embedded in my uniform and faced the same direction as T-Fal.

The robot raised one arm and pointed at the wall. A beam of light came out from the end and projected onto the white laminate cabinet. I'd expected to see the recording of Pika that was already a permanent part of my photographic memory banks and was surprised when the image was of my dad. He was looking at T-Fal's access panel. A light, coming out from inside T-Fal, reflected off his purple face.

"Help me out here, robot," my dad said. "Where is your medical data filed?"

"Medical records stored in data bank three. Medical procedure instructions stored in data bank four," T-Fal said. "Keyword search recommended."

"Access data bank four."

Given the choice between medical history or procedures, he'd chosen procedures. That told me he wanted T-Fal to perform a task. Was he already hurt when this took place? T-Fal had been left in security section to monitor the grey prisoners and my dad, so he'd presumably been down there when whatever it was that happened had happened. And as I scanned the background, it became clear that the holding cell was where they were. But where were the greys? Sure, they could be huddled in a corner off screen, but even that spoke to them being present while this took place, and if the greys were capable of killing Mattix and sabotaging the ship, I doubted they'd stand by and watch a Plunian rewire a robot and not interfere.

Yet it didn't appear as though T-Fal was doing anything other than following commands like a normal robot would. Whoever had programmed him—Kentaro, by my best guess—would have written his code. Simple yes/no sequences, search capabilities, tasks to complete when the requests were activated. Aside from his nonstick Teflon surface, T-Fal wasn't all that different from Cat. What was it my dad wanted him to do?

"Keyword search recommended," T-Fal repeated, prompting a command.

"Keyword Search: download instruction manual for medical procedure five point three two three."

That was interesting. Dad knew the medical code for whatever it was he wanted done. Had he sustained an injury he'd experienced before? Was he sick? What was medical procedure 5.323?

The knowledge I had from memorizing the BOP wouldn't help me with this. Medical had a separate manual, the M-BOP. I turned away from the projection and scanned the interior of Medi-Bay until I spotted the computer on the far wall by the antiseptic swabs. I quickly retrieved it and resumed my position, hoping I hadn't missed much of the digital file. I held the computer tablet in the air above the body cam and accessed the file manager, tuning out the digital imaging while I typed in keywords to find a match in the database.

Lights and sounds from T-Fal's projection caught my attention. I looked up. Blue, red, and white pulses from the robot blinked against my dad's skin. Clicking and whirring sounds replaced the robot's speech. Seconds later, the lights and sounds stopped. "Search complete.

Download procedure to active files? Yes or no."

"Yes."

"File downloaded. Run program? Yes or no."

"Yes."

My dad had rewired the robot to recognize his voice and follow his verbal commands. He appeared to be prepping T-Fal for something, but I didn't know what. Did this have to do with the navigation of the ship? Overriding the coordinates to Saturn? Was he the one keeping us from getting there?

Did that mean my dad was a murderer?

"Command in queue. Assume position for diagnostic prep calibrations."

My dad straightened up and faced T-Fal. "Position assumed."

A red light pulsed out of the robot and swept my dad from top to bottom. "Scanning measurements. Measurements complete. Calibrating procedure. Calibration complete. Rotate 180 degrees." My dad turned to the far wall with his back facing the robot. The red light came back and repeated the diagnostics. When the computer was done, it said, "Launch program with verbal command."

"Launch program," my dad said.

I scrolled through lists of medical procedures to find the one my dad had programmed, and when my finger rested on 5.323, a wave of nausea and fear swept over me. I looked up, horrified, at what I knew was about to take place.

My dad tipped his head forward with his chin down toward his chest. A white light slowly rose up the back of his uniform and rested on the center of his neck. The light sliced into his purple flesh at the base of his head and a retractor extended out of T-Fal's arm until it was pressed up against my dad's spinal cord. Right at the point of impact of Doc's chipping gun.

My dad had programmed T-Fal to remove the tracking chip. I already knew about chip removal. It was illegal. It was dangerous. And there was a less than 10 percent chance of survival in those who had the nerve to try.

24: GALAXY NEWS SERVICE

I closed my eyes. I didn't have to watch the surgical procedure. I could picture my dad's body on the floor of the holding cell with blood running out from under his head. That blood must have come from the exit wound inflicted by T-Fal. The procedure was not without pain or complications, even if performed by a robot.

And I'd called Doc to attend to him. The man who had shot the tracking chip into his neck had, by now, discovered he'd had it removed. With Kentaro assisting. Would the medic recognize his robot had performed the surgery?

Worst yet: what did this say about my dad's innocence or guilt?

"Neptune," I said. "Can you hear me?"

"Go."

"There's video in T-Fal showing my dad had T-Fal remove the tracking chip from his head. The operation was done in the holding cell. I don't know where the greys are because they're not on the video."

"You need to erase that file from the robot."

"But—"

"Evidence that Jack Stryker tampered with Federation Council security measures is ground for termination."

Termination didn't mean losing his job. Termination was a fancy word for government-sanctioned murder.

"What do you think Doc is going to do?"

"His oath requires him treat the patient. After that, I don't know."

I'd wanted Neptune to offer words of comfort, but I knew he wouldn't lie to spare my feelings. I felt helpless.

"I'm going to take T-Fal to the uniform ward. There might be more information embedded in his data files, but I don't want to be in Medi-Bay when Doc and Kentaro get back. Stryker out."

T-Fal was on wheels, which made it easy for me to maneuver him out of Medi-Bay, through the corridor, and into the uniform ward. There was no reason for me to bring him here other than it was roomy. Nobody from Moon Unit Corporation was going to check to see if I kept the crew of Moon Unit Mini 7.2 dressed to code because nobody from Moon Unit Corporation knew we were on the ship.

That thought gave me pause. Somebody *had* to have noticed a missing ship by now. Originally Neptune had planned to use warp speed and get us to Saturn and back before the ship was found missing. But the structural damage to the ship from earlier dictated we play it safe and fly the ship at normal speeds. We'd been gone for a day, and sure, probably had a head start of a couple of hours before the crime became known, but what measures would they take to find us? They had to have the ability to communicate with the ship or locate us on their home base navigational panel. You can't just steal a spaceship and expect no one to notice.

I signed into the uniform ward computer and hacked into the Galaxy News Service. The GNS maintained satellites throughout the Milky Way and reported on all sorts of news stories, both those built on facts and those built on speculation. I could have pulled up the last five issues and scanned the headlines, but by hacking into the backend of their interface, I could quickly determine which of their recent stories had garnered the most response and outrage. Surely a stolen Moon Unit Mini Series 7 would be in there.

It wasn't in there.

Moon Unit Corporation had ample time to discover the missing Moon Unit Mini 7.2. They had time to activate the Galaxy Positioning System to pinpoint our whereabouts. They had time to contact the space police and report a missing ship, or file charges of grand theft spaceship, or radio in to our communications officer and demand we turn the ship around and return to the docking station.

They'd done none of that. Why not?

It wasn't mentioned anywhere in the list of recently published articles, or trending topics, or warnings, or notices of criminal activity. It was as if we'd gotten away with it. But I didn't believe that to be possible.

I pulled a fresh prototype uniform out of the closet. This one came to mid-thigh and was paired with webbed tights designed for maximum flexibility and movement and minimal bulk. I unzipped the soiled uniform I wore and tossed it into the laundry bin, removed my gravity boots, and pulled on the tights. I'd forgotten to switch on the manual gravity and slowly I rose through the air. My old uniform was the only one in the laundry bin when I tossed it there, and now it, too, floated up to the ceiling. Other items were secured and remained in place.

T-Fal must have been programmed to detect changes in gravitational pull because he stayed on the carpeted floor. I wriggled around a bit until the tights were tight in all the right places and realized the rest of the uniform was floating on the other side of the room. I pushed my foot off the wall and glided across the room to the uniform. I had barely gotten it over my head when the doors swished open.

Rebel Rune entered. He looked side to side, his eyes shifty. He glanced at the uniform closet and T-Fal. The closet was closed and T-Fal was inactive. To Rune, it might have appeared that he'd been rolled here for storage.

Rune was still wearing his original uniform and his gravity boots, so he remained on the ground. In trying to determine what brought him here, I reached one conclusion: he'd come to terms with our mission and wanted to suit up like Ivi and Kentaro. Floating above him was a pretty good way to undermine any credibility I may have established, so I kept myself lodged by the ceiling with the toe of my foot hooked under a security strap. When he figured out I wasn't there and wasn't coming back, he'd leave. At least that's what I expected.

But he didn't leave. He approached the computer and pressed his palm onto the touchpad. The light scanned it and followed with the ocular scan. Even from my position by the ceiling, I could tell the computer unlocked and gave him access to the same Galaxy News Service that I'd been mining moments before.

Whatever Rune was doing in the uniform ward, it had nothing to do with uniforms.

25: THE VIEW FROM ABOVE

Rune searched the news network. For the briefest moment, the lack of information on our crime seemed to be a blessing. Until Rune pulled a flat disc out of his pocket and inserted it into the computer drive. Was he downloading files? Uploading falsified information? Sending a coded message that he was a hostage aboard the Moon Unit Mini 7.2?

I couldn't have cared less about the flexibility of the new prototype uniform tights. What this uniform needed was a magnification shield to allow me to see what was happening across the room. If I made a noise, he'd hear it. If I moved, he'd see me. There was nothing for me to do.

"Stryker," Neptune's voice in my comm device startled me, and I flinched. I pressed my lips together and kept quiet. A few moments passed. "Stryker. Report." I didn't say a word. *"Stryker!"*

Crap. Neptune meant business. But it was clear to me

that whatever Rune was doing, he wasn't doing under Neptune's orders and from my unique vantage point, I was the only one who would know. There's something to be said for taking your gravity boots off every once in a while.

Rune removed the disc from the computer. He slipped it into his uniform pocket and left. I counted to five and when Rune didn't return, called out to T-Fal to help me down.

"T-Fal, activate gravity switch."

T-Fal lit up, and he pivoted in a half circle. His arm extended, and he rolled to the wall.

The doors opened. Neptune stormed in with Cat under his arm, barely missing a collision with the robot. Unfortunately, when T-Fal activated the gravity switch on the wall, I crashed down from the ceiling, so Neptune's entrance wasn't entirely collision-free.

Neptune dropped Cat and caught me. His arms were strong and secure and didn't let go right away. Cat landed on the carpet and rocked side to side with lights flashing. I wriggled out of Neptune's arms and scooped Cat off the floor. I tugged the hem of my short uniform down with my spare hand. When I looked at Neptune, he was looking up.

"What were you doing?"

I wasn't about to admit something as foolish as putting my uniform on in mid-air, so I avoided the unimportant question and went with more pressing matters.

"Rebel Rune was in here. He accessed my computer. At first, it looked like he wanted to see my recent files but then he put a disc in the computer drive and did something. I was too far away to see if he uploaded or downloaded or sent a message."

"You were in the air."

"Turns out it's a pretty good spot for surveillance."

Neptune looked inside the laundry bin. When T-Fal turned the gravity back on, my old uniform had fallen back inside. A clue that I'd changed. Neptune checked the uniform closet. The inventory was neatly folded and organized. A clue that I'd maintained the proper ward standards even though this wasn't a real trip. He turned to T-Fal. "Report on Lieutenant Stryker's behavior."

"Lieutenant Stryker arrived in uniform ward at Zulu Twenty-two. Lieutenant Stryker accessed the Galaxy News Service via the uniform computer. Lieutenant Stryker changed into a new prototype uniform. Recording of Lieutenant Stryker's actions lost when Lieutenant Stryker went out of range."

"Up," Neptune said.

"Up," I repeated.

"Exact location of Lieutenant Stryker lost for seventeen minutes. Presence of Lieutenant Stryker now confirmed in uniform ward."

"That's enough, T-Fal," Neptune said. The robot's lights blinked off. "Turn around," Neptune said to me.

Turn around? I turned. I searched the room for

whatever it was that Neptune wanted me to see. I felt his hands tug the back of my uniform together and then raise the zipper until it was shut. A flush ran through me.

I turned back to face him. "I came in here to change, okay? And I forgot to turn on the gravity because I was wearing my gravity boots, but when I took them off I floated up into the air and that's as good a place as any to get dressed. When Rune came in and didn't see me, he mistakenly thought he was alone and I kept my presence secret because I don't trust him. If I had answered you, the sound would have given me away."

I stood tall and confident. I knew floating around in the top of the uniform ward seemed silly to him, but it had worked. I'd gotten important intel that we wouldn't have if not for that.

Neptune crossed his arms. I waited for a lecture and then got tired of waiting and jumped in. "Mattix Dusk is dead. Pika is missing. There are grey aliens on board the ship and a crew member—my dad—who may be dying in a holding cell in security section. Do you think me forgetting to turn on the gravity is our biggest problem?"

"What were you looking for on the GNS?"

"I thought somebody would be after us by now. We stole a Moon Unit. Even if it was a Series 7, it's a spaceship. We. Stole. A. Spaceship." I held my hands up in front of me. "I'm not pointing any fingers here, but isn't that weird? Shouldn't there be enforcers after us? This ship must have a signal so the Moon Unit Corporation can find us via remote radio control or contact us in case of trouble."

"You expected to find that in the GNS?"

"No. I hacked into their database and looked at the most commented upon articles in the past twenty-four hours. If anybody cared that we took the ship, they'd put out a warning about us, right? How do they know the Moon Unit Mini 7.2 isn't under pirate control right now?"

"Moon Unit Corporation knows where we are and why we took the ship," he said.

Say what?

"I can't tell you any more than I have," Neptune said. "You said Rune accessed your computer."

I nodded. "I didn't expect anybody else to come in here. I would have wiped the recent activity logs before I left, but when I floated up and he walked in, there wasn't time."

"He knows what you were looking at."

"Yes." Now that I was back on the ground, I went to the computer and cued it up. Like me, Rune hadn't wiped the activity log. Whatever he'd done, I might be able to undo it. I unlocked the computer, stood still for the ocular scan, and, with a few keystrokes, knew exactly what Rune had needed my computer for.

I turned to Neptune. "Rune wiped the existing navigational charts from the computer. We're freefalling through space. The only way we'll make it to Saturn is if somebody takes manual control and flies us there. And the only person who can do that is Rune." There was a rumble under my feet. I felt the ship jerk and then looked up to see if Neptune had noticed it too.

He pushed me aside and activated the computer. "Computer, requesting immediate diagnostic report of Moon Unit Mini 7.2."

"Moon Unit Mini 7.2 diagnostic report. All systems go. Escape hatch open. Emergency pod engaged. Departure imminent."

"Show me escape hatch," he said.

The computer flickered to a new screen that showed Rebel Rune strapped into the single escape pod that the Moon Unit Mini had been equipped with. We stood, helpless, while the pod designed to fly at least ten of us to safety glided out of the escape hatch and into the blackness of the sky. Bright orange and blue flames appeared from the two solid rocket boosters, propelling the pod away until a blast shot it far enough to be little more than a speck in the sky.

"He's gone," I said. "Rune just went AWOL and he took the only emergency pod on the ship. He was our pilot."

"Not our only pilot," Neptune said. "There's another qualified spaceship pilot on board the ship."

Jack Stryker was our last hope—if he survived.

26: A LITTLE BIT OF HISTORY REPEATING

I would not ignore what led us to this moment and waste time sulking. I'd learned a long time ago that I was responsible for my actions, and if I'd graduated and gotten a job in the security sector as I'd hoped, I'd be responsible for others' actions as well. Jack Stryker was the most qualified person for the job we needed filled and he was on the ship. If he were anybody else, I wouldn't give the decision a second thought.

And deep down, I knew if I needed him to prove his innocence to me, this was a heck of an opportunity.

"His health—the last time I saw him—he was fading in and out of consciousness in the holding cell. There's a digital recording on T-Fal that indicates my dad programmed the robot to remove the tracking chip."

"Doc shot that chip into Jack. He's going to know what happened."

"I know."

Neptune turned to the intercom on the wall. "Neptune to Doc. Come in, Doc."

Doc's surly voice responded over the intercom. "What do you want? And let's try to keep the captain stuff to a minimum."

"I need a status report on Jack Stryker."

"Is Lieutenant Stryker with you?"

Neptune looked at me. I shook my head. "No," he said.

"The convict is recovering in Medi-Bay, where he'll be under my supervision until we land on Saturn. A member of Federation Council will meet us at the landing coordinates. He'll take him into custody and transport him to Colony 13."

The whole situation had a sickening familiarity to it. But this time, I would be privy to the events as they unfolded. Last time, Federation Police came to Plunia, unannounced, and invaded our home. Interrupted our dinner. Bound my dad's hands behind his back and took him away like a common criminal. I'd barely understood the charges. My mom had sent me out of the room to keep me from watching, but instead I'd stood in the MPs path and yelled at the uniformed men to leave us alone. They had the wrong planet. They had the wrong house. They had the wrong man.

When the news broke the following day, the evidence was overwhelmingly clear. Jack Stryker had entered into an agreement with space pirate Cheung Qidd to restrict the delivery of dry ice to planets throughout the galaxy. Those planets suffered from a lack of oxygen. Inhabitants got sick. Some died. Qidd's cronies raped and pillaged. They destroyed what little commerce existed. And when the inhabitants had nothing left, Qidd offered oxygen relief for slavery, thus owning the culture he'd destroyed. It was no wonder my mom and I had been outcast.

And here I was, reliving it all over again. Different pirate in charge, but the same threat and same danger. The only difference was this time I was a criminal too. Like father, like daughter.

I shook the thoughts away and refocused on Neptune. He was watching me. I buried my emotions deep inside and concentrated on what I knew. Point: we needed my dad to pilot the ship. Point: Doc had no plans to release him from custody. Point: without a pilot, we were little more than a ship of crew and Gremlons hurling through space on a collision course with the biggest planet in the galaxy.

And then, Doc added, "Tell Lieutenant Stryker this bears no reflection on her."

"Done," Neptune said. "Neptune out."

I didn't know what to expect from Neptune and I didn't wait to hear it. I pulled on my gravity boots and headed for the exit. Neptune grabbed my arm and spun me toward him.

"I have to talk to him," I said. After three long seconds, Neptune let go of my arm and I left.

***

Under normal circumstances, Medi-Bay was an oasis on a spaceship. Enforced procedure and codes of ethics didn't apply. Doc was in charge and it was his choice to act formally or casually. I wasn't sure which way things would go.

Doc stood over a long, silver surface typing information into his computer. When I entered, he turned the monitor off and put the computer back on the wall.

"I need to talk to you," I said. "In confidence."

"Sylvia, my hands are tied. If I could look the other way for you, I would, but there's too much at stake."

"There's too much at stake if you keep him locked up."

Doc eyed me with suspicion. I wasn't going to blow my only chance to convince him to hear me out. He turned his back on me and I felt my window of opportunity closing. "Doc, wait!" I said. "If we don't have his help, we're all going to die."

Doc hesitated at the back of Medi-Bay. He pressed a button on the wall and a light went on over the door that separated Medi-Bay from the Medi-Morgue. A matching light was above the door I'd entered. Doc picked up two padded stools. He set them down, held his hand out to one, and then sat on the other.

"I'm a doctor, not an officer. You can speak freely and without fear of repercussion."

"Why are you here?" I asked.

"I told you why. The scheduler fouled up."

"I don't believe you." He looked angry. "You're too smart. You wouldn't have just shown up. You would have verified the scheduler or contacted Moon Unit Corporation or something. I know you want me to believe it was coincidence, but I'm sorry. I have too much respect for you to believe you did something so obtuse."

"How about you tell me what all this is about first?"

I didn't have much of a choice. "This isn't an approved Moon Unit trip. A courier from Colony 5 was murdered on a routine trip to Saturn. He took Pika with him—you remember Ensign Pika, right? The Gremlon who was on Moon Unit 5 and 6?"

He nodded.

"She recorded a message on my robot Cat and sent him with Mattix on his return ship. But when the Dusk Driver arrived, Mattix was dead. I think—Neptune and I think—Omicron Faarstar is behind the murder and the kidnapping. If Pika is still alive, she's being held hostage. We borrowed the Moon Unit to rescue her."

"Borrowed?"

I smiled feebly. "I posted last minute jobs on the Moon Unit message board. The crew you see all answered that ad."

"You required them to show up with medical clearance," he said, matching the facts he knew with the information I provided. "That's why I had a sudden influx of last-minute tests."

"Which made you suspicious. I get that. What I don't get is why you showed up with your gear bag and willingly got on a ship that you had no official word you were supposed to get on."

This time I waited for a response. Doc's role in all of this was too pivotal. I'd committed a criminal act too. If I had to, I'd strike a deal with him: two Strykers for the price of one when we landed. I'd say anything I had to say to get him to release my dad so he could pilot the plane, including the fact that not doing so was certain death for all of us—him included.

Doc's shoulders slumped, and he stared at a spot on the floor. When he did finally speak, it wasn't what I expected. And the truth was something I never could have predicted.

27: DOUBLE AGENT

Doc looked up from the ground to my face. He bit his lip as if trying to keep from talking, but ultimately the silence was too much for him to bear.

"After the last two trips, Moon Unit Corporation called me for a performance review. Turns out it's not such a feather in your cap to have passengers or crew members die on your watch. I was put on probation."

He stood up and went to a cabinet in the back of the room. Out came a bottle of whiskey and two glasses. He poured a finger full in each glass and carried them back to the chairs. I took one of the glasses but didn't take a sip. Doc did.

"I had a medical practice on Earth. Lost everything over a malpractice suit. The only reason I'm in space is because I needed the kind of fresh start that doesn't come around every day and Moon Unit Corporation offered that."

"That's why a lot of people took this job."

"Not exactly. Do you know much about Moon Units 1-4?"

"I know about 1-3. I haven't been able to find anything on Moon Unit 4. It's classified."

"Well, that's comforting. If you can't find anything out, then nobody can." He gave me a wry smile. "Knowing you as I do, I'm guessing you didn't just flip a couple of rocks."

"I may have looked harder than that."

"These ships have had trouble. Internal trouble. When the original company sold and the new owners took over and reorganized, they thought they were in the clear. New business model, different target audience. Diversify. Offer people the trip of a lifetime. And then Moon Unit 6 and that trouble with Venus."

Understatement of the year!

That trip had exposed a secret government experiment on babies born in a lab and delivered a Venusian slave to freedom. Not to mention almost getting me killed a few times.

"Doc, you saved my life on that trip. I made my report and submitted a written record for you to receive a commendation."

"I know. And that's what makes what I'm about to tell you all the more difficult." He finished his whiskey and set the glass on the floor by the wheel of his cart. "I appreciate your commendation. I know it came from a decent place and that you meant to do something good, and for that I thank you."

"But...?"

"But I didn't record your treatment in my medical records. It was a legitimate procedure, but for reasons that only those of us who were on that trip will ever fully understand, I thought it might be prudent to keep the details to myself."

He didn't have to explain further. My good deed had raised a red flag. If I'd needed emergency medical treatment, then why hadn't Doc reported it? What else took place on a Moon Unit that wasn't being reported? I could only imagine how the company would view his independent decision.

"I didn't realize what would happen," I said.

"I know. Neither did I. But in cases like these, when someone scratches the surface and finds something they didn't expect, they dig deeper. They draw conclusions. They form theories and they lay blame and suspicions start to grow."

"Suspicions of what? You did everything right. And they already know who was responsible for the murders on both treks, right? I solved both cases for them. They should be thanking me and thanking you for saving me."

"They think someone on their payroll is responsible for their trouble. They put me through a rigorous interview process to determine what involvement, if any, I may have had."

"Moon Unit Corporation thinks you had something to do with the murders on the ship?"

"No. Moon Unit Corporation suspects someone entirely different and they've got me on the hook to spy."

"On me?" I asked incredulously.

"No. On the security ape pretending to be captain. Moon Unit Corporation's got it in for Neptune."

28: TO TRUST OR NOT TO TRUST

I sat in stunned silence. Neptune was the only person on the ship that I trusted and here was Doc telling me our employer thought he was behind multiple murders and classified horrors that I hadn't been able to uncover even with above-my-pay-grade hacking abilities.

It explained a lot. It explained why Doc was here. It explained why he didn't trust Neptune acting as captain. It explained why we'd been able to walk off with a spaceship and nobody at the company questioned who had lifted the keys. They thought they knew who was responsible. And then Neptune had arranged for Jack Stryker, known criminal, to be on board. It explained why Doc chipped Jack and planned to turn him over to Federation Council when we landed.

Doc's actions were intended to prove his loyalty and cooperation.

And Neptune was going to take the fall.

I swallowed a gulp of Doc's whiskey. The sharp taste burned the back of my throat and my eyes watered. I set the glass on the floor and looked up. "You agreed to do a job. I'm not going to waste time talking you out of doing it. But we have a whole other issue that you need to understand."

Doc watched me. He'd said a lot, more than I'd ever heard him say on both moon treks combined, and if I let him stop and think, he'd probably question his decision to confide in me. But I had no intention of letting him stop and think.

"We're on a rescue mission, but our pilot, Rebel Rune, just took off with the emergency pod. Which means we're one person down and there's no way off the ship until we reach Saturn. We have grey aliens roaming the halls. I think they came on board when we materialized the Gremlons, but I can't be sure. They were in the holding cell with my dad before"—I froze—"before his injury," I finished. I paused to give Doc time to react, verbally or with body language. I could read a lot out of both thanks to specialty courses at the academy. Doc didn't move. He didn't tense up. What he did was lean forward, hanging on my every word.

"Doc, the greys have numbers tattooed on their hands."

"The mark of Omicron Faarstar."

I nodded. "If he's behind the murder, the hostage situation, and the turbulence we thought we sustained that could have destroyed the ship, then he needs to be brought to justice. Ensign Pika is a witness to what he did. We need her to testify."

Doc laughed. "Justice," he repeated. "Funny word coming from you."

"We need my dad to pilot the ship," I said quietly. All the other details, suspicions, and fears were immaterial. "Ivi and Kentaro have been briefed and are willing to help. You already arranged for a representative from Federation Council to take my dad into custody when we arrive on Saturn. They can arrest me too; I won't fight. Let him do this one thing before he returns to jail for the rest of his life."

"You were trained for this sort of thing. I've picked up that much. What are the risks?"

"The risks of not using him are pretty high."

"And you trust him? You know what he was accused of. You know what happened to your planet. His actions led to your mother's—and your whole race's—annihilation. I know Plunians are unemotional, but come on, Sylvia. You can just let that go?"

I looked down at my hands, sure that if I made eye contact my speech would falter. "I can't do anything about the lives that were already lost." I looked up at Doc. "But if we don't do this—if you don't allow him to do this—then the lives lost on this ship will be on your head."

We were both quiet. I would not be the first to speak. As precious moments ticked off and Doc possibly cursed the decision to show up for this trip, I sat as still as a droid with no power source.

"I'll escort Jack Stryker to the bridge at Zulu Six tomorrow morning." He stood. "What about Neptune?"

I stood too. "What about Neptune?" I repeated, not sure what he was asking.

"Be careful, Sylvia," Doc said. "That guy will say what he needs to say to get you to trust him."

I didn't respond. I was about to leave when a voice sounded in my ear. "Make sure your dad's in uniform."

Darn that comm device! There was no reason for Neptune to remind me to outfit my dad in a Moon Unit uniform. Not now. There was only one reason he had. He'd heard everything Doc said, and he wanted to make sure I knew.

I ran to the uniform ward. The door was open. I grabbed the next available uniform from the men's side and slammed the door shut. Yoka, the boy Gremlon, was hiding on the other side of the door. I screamed. He shrank by about 20 percent.

"Did I scare you?" he asked.

"Yes. Did you follow me?"

"I was here," he said. "When you were in the air." He pointed up to the corner of the ceiling where I'd floated. "And when the giant hollered at you. I hid so you wouldn't see me."

"That's not possible. How were you here?"

"I rode in the robot."

"Show me."

Yoka trembled. He shrank more, and his normally pointy ears flattened themselves back against his otherwise round pink head. I'd watched Pika do this many times and would never get used to it.

"Yoka, you're not in trouble."

He zipped across the room. Darn it! I had to talk in positive words only. Negatives were bad words to Gremlons, and by the looks of Yoka he was ready to run away from home to avoid being punished. "Do you remember Pika? My friend?" Yoka nodded. His eyes were wide. "She liked playing with Cat. I think she was friends with T-Fal too."

"She was," he said. "She told me how to hide in him."

"When?"

"When she talked to me."

"When did Pika talk to you?"

"This morning. She came to my room and we talked about what it was like on Saturn and she told me to tell you she was okay but she can't let you know where she is."

"Pika is still on Saturn," I said. And then I stopped to think. "Isn't she?"

Yoka was instantly excited that he knew something I didn't. He crept forward, and his ears perked up. "Can't tell can't tell can't tell," he said.

"Will you show me how to hide in T-Fal?" I asked him.

He put his hands behind his back and pushed his

round pink belly out toward me.

"I'll give you a uniform," I said.

"Like yours?"

I glanced at mine. It was the prototype yellow and white shift with white reinforced tights. I couldn't outfit Yoka in this uniform, but I could give him one of the other prototypes. "It'll be close to mine, okay?"

"Okay! After," he said.

"After what?"

He walked up to T-Fal and wrapped his arms around the robot's base. It looked like he was giving the robot a hug. But his nimble fingers explored buttons and rivets and within seconds, the front of T-Fal's cylindrical base raised.

A hidden compartment. Who knew?

Somebody. Because the compartment wasn't empty. Inside was the body of a dead grey alien with a 3 tattooed on his hand. And if a grey was responsible for murdering Mattix, then who was responsible for murdering a grey?

29: AND THINGS GET WORSE

"Uh-oh!" Yoka said. He zipped to the other side of the room and hid behind the cabinet door.

I backed away from T-Fal until I felt the edge of the bench pressing into my calves. This was not good. This was not good on many, many, many levels. I could think of only one person to call.

"Neptune, I need you in the uniform ward. Now," I said.

The doors opened, and Neptune came in. He didn't acknowledge what he'd heard Doc tell me, and right now we had bigger problems. I didn't ask why he'd been so close. It didn't matter. I pointed to T-Fal and the open panel without saying a word. Neptune approached the robot and touched the tip of his boot to the dead alien inside. Grey Three disintegrated into a pile of ash that Neptune quickly removed with the vacuum setting on his gun.

Fact: There were greys on board the ship.

Fact: Neptune had killed a grey alien on his property. The grey alien who had escaped from the Dusk Driver.

Fact: A grey alien had tried to kill me in engineering.

Fact: Yoka knew of the presence of the grey in T-Fal.

Fact: We were likely screwed.

"Yoka?" I said. I pointed to the closet door so Neptune knew we weren't alone. "Can you come say hi to Pika's friend Neptune?"

Yoka peeked out from behind the door. His eyes were wide. "The giant is here?"

That's what Pika called him. And that's when I knew he'd been telling the truth about her, about talking to her, about her teaching him how to hide in T-Fal.

"Okay okay okay," Yoka said. He crept forward, wrapped his hands around T-Fal, pressed some buttons, and the door slid down.

"Take T-Fal to my quarters," I said to Neptune.

"You don't have quarters."

"You know, *my quarters*. We were in them earlier today. My stuff was there, and you told me that's where I would be staying tonight, so they must be my quarters. Is any of this ringing a bell?"

Neptune closed his eyes for a moment as if something in the room required extra patience on his part. When he opened them, he glared at me. "Meet me in *your quarters* in five minutes."

"Sure thing," I said.

I let Neptune leave first and then turned to Yoka. "Do you know where Pika is?"

He nodded.

"Can you tell me?"

He shook his head.

"Even if it's really really really important?"

"Really really really?"

"Really really really."

He shook his head again.

"Can you ask Pika if it's okay if you tell me? Can you tell her I said it was really really really important?"

He nodded.

I didn't think I was going to get much more than that.

I pulled the prototype uniform out of the closet and handed it to the scared alien boy. "Put this on," I said, and then I left. No point wasting time now.

By the time I arrived at Neptune's quarters, the five minutes were up. T-Fal was roaming the hallway.

"Hello, Lieutenant Stryker. The captain is anticipating your arrival."

"I'm sure he is," I said under my breath. I slapped my hand on the door and it opened.

Cat sat on the table facing Neptune with his head tipped back, making it look like he was gazing up at Neptune. A meow on repeat sounded from Cat's mechanical mouth.

Neptune turned to me. "Make this thing stop."

"What did you do? He only meows when something

bothers him."

"I don't know. He was meowing when I got here. He's probably been meowing for hours. Why am I calling it a him?"

"Because I call him a him and Pika calls him a him and you got used to it."

I picked Cat up and examined him. His eyes scanned mine, and when his internal data chip matched them to my digital override code, he went silent. I set him back on the table and turned to Neptune.

"We have problems. Multiple problems. I'm going to list them to the best of my ability. We need to prioritize and tackle them one at a time. There is no room for personal vendettas."

He studied me, his dark focused eyes moving back and forth between my own. "Go."

"Someone on this ship killed a grey and stuffed the body in T-Fal. Was it you?"

Neptune kept his eyes on me. He didn't move a muscle. Not even the big ones in his biceps. "What do you think?"

"You had opportunity. You knew Grey Three and Four were in the holding cell because you put them there. You killed Grey One before we took off. You have been around T-Fal enough to be able to put the body in him. And your regular job as the head of security puts you in a position to eliminate any threats to the passengers on board the ship. Grey aliens are known threats to the ship."

"Your assessment is that I did it."

"Not so fast. I didn't know T-Fal had a hidden compartment. It's possible that you didn't know it either. Yoka said Pika taught him and the only way that's possible is if Pika is on this ship."

"You think Pika is on the ship?"

Cat's eyes lit up and he meowed again. The meows were insistent. There was no ignoring him. And being the person who had built him from scratch and programmed his alarm codes, I realized he'd been trying to tell Neptune something when I walked in.

"Cat," I said. "He carried the message from Pika. She knows how to work him. She knew how to get him to record and save the message and who knows what else."

I turned around and faced the robot cat. "Cat. Where is Pika?"

Cat's head tipped back again, and his eyes lit up. The beam of light blinked repeatedly. "It's code," I said.

Neptune joined me. The blinking lights flashed out a message, paused, and then repeated the sequence. It had been a long time since I'd studied code breaking courses, but the message was clear. *SOS. Pika is with Faarstar.*

The coded message didn't fit with what Yoka had told me. And I had been sure that Yoka had been telling the truth. I looked at Neptune. He looked at me. He turned back to Cat. "Is Faarstar on our ship?"

I repeated the question and Cat's blinking lights doubled in speed. *Affirmative.*

30: GOTTA MAKE A LIVING

"Faarstar is here?" I asked out loud. "On the Moon Unit? With us?"

Cat's eyes blinked code again.

"How accurate is Cat's intel?" Neptune asked.

"Cat is a robot. He knows what he's been programmed to know and what he's confirmed through data. Until we found that recording from Pika, I didn't think anybody else knew how to program him. Except you." I held his stare. "Yes, I know you deleted the files I stole from the border patrol agent on the trip to Venus. You didn't know I already read them, did you? I know you worked as a bounty hunter before you joined Moon Unit Corp. No judgment. Everybody's gotta make a living."

"Tell me about Mattix Dusk," Neptune said.

"We're not going to talk about you? About your past? I told you my deepest secret and you still don't trust me?"

I wanted—needed—Neptune's reassurance that we were partners. No secrets. His silence stung in a way I wasn't prepared for, and I felt a wall go up inside of me. "You already know about Mattix. He's a courier. He picks up and delivers merchandise between planets. I met him after Moon Unit 5 and he taught me how to fight in exchange for repairs on his ship."

"I find it hard to believe he didn't do his own repairs."

"He probably could do most things, but he wanted some extras."

"Extras?"

"Rear projection, extended range on his buffer zone, additional languages in his translator. Stuff like that."

"Extras."

"Mattix delivered a priority package to Zeke Champion's dad, Hubble. You remember Zeke, right? He helped us with the trip to Venus?"

"I know who Zeke Champion is."

Little by little, Neptune's small circle had expanded thanks to the people I'd befriended in my life. Zeke Champion had been my study partner at Space Academy before I'd dropped out. He was the son of Hubble Champion, a spaceship repairman, and he'd never met a computer he couldn't hack. Without his help, Neptune and my last mission would have failed.

"Then you remember Zeke's dad repairs drones. I made a deal with Zeke that I'd repair the busted drones on Hubble's property in exchange for room and board.

Mattix delivered a package of drone parts to Hubble. While Mattix was waiting for payment, he asked if I had any experience with space pods. I told him I could work on anything electronic or computerized, and we worked out a deal."

"You make a lot of deals," he said.

"A girl's gotta make a living too."

"You make a lot of deals *with men,*" he clarified.

"Men happen to be the ones willing to pay for my services."

"How do you know it wasn't a trap?"

"What kind of trap? I supercharged his space pod and he taught me to fight like a girl. Seems fair to me."

Neptune leaned closer and I leaned back. It was a rookie mistake. I'd just indicated intimidation. I returned to erect posture, which brought our faces inches from each other.

"You sold yourself short," he said.

"I didn't have any other choices. Oh, wait. I did have one, but it involved my other unique quality, and I've never been interested in selling the experience of sleeping with a purple woman for money. And trust me, men have offered to pay for that as well."

Neptune grabbed my arm and shook me. "Don't let me hear you say that again."

"Why? After my dad was arrested, that's all people thought I was good for. When Qidd started accumulating slaves, what do you think he did with them? Rumor has it he kept a harem on every planet. I've found sources that said when he was arrested, there was a bounty on me. A group of students at the academy sent a signal into the galaxy offering to deliver me to the highest bidder. So yes, the fights I got into at Space Academy were raw and clumsy and fueled by rage. Nobody's left to take care of me, Neptune. *That's* why I repaired Mattix's space pod. I wanted to learn how to fight so I could take care of myself."

Neptune slipped his arm around my waist and pulled me up against him. "I can teach you more than Mattix Dusk pretended to know," he said in a low voice. "and we both know how you can pay me back."

I thought about meeting Neptune on Moon Unit 5. In our first conversation, he brought up my dad. When he arrested me, he made a crack about taking me to Colony 13 where my dad and I could share a cell. At one point he'd even told me he knew more about me than I thought. I hadn't questioned any of that and now those memories haunted me.

Neptune was the most isolated person I'd ever met, but he'd made room in his life for me and a part of me had always wondered why.

But now, with his strong arms holding me against him in the privacy of his quarters, my self-preservation instincts went on red alert. For the first time since I'd acknowledged my attraction to Neptune, his nearness didn't make me glow or flush and I knew why. He was after a bounty. He was never going to take me into his confidence.

Neptune could take whatever he wanted and right now, he wanted me. And whatever respect I'd developed for him since that first moon trek crumbled. He was just like the rest of the galaxy. Looking to make a trade for my services.

The sting of Neptune's betrayal left me cold. I pushed against his chest. The effort wasn't enough to force him to release me, but he did. I stepped back, keeping my eyes on him.

"Why are we still going to Saturn?" I asked Neptune. "Mattix is dead. We can't bring him back. We thought we were going to save Pika, but I think she's on the ship. If we go there, we're just going to take her back to danger. We need to turn the ship around and go back to the spaceship hangar. Rune was the only smart one on the ship. No good is going to come from us landing on Saturn."

"You don't know what you're talking about."

"Yes, I do. You're just like everybody else. This teachable moment nonsense is one more way for you to control me." I pointed to my head. "And this comm device in my ear? That's not being a mentor. That's being a stalker. How do you think it feels to know you know who I talk to, what I say, and when I say it? That's not a partnership, Neptune. That's just creepy. If you don't turn this ship around, I'll get my dad to do it."

"Stryker," he said.

"Yes. Stryker." I moved my hand back and forth

between us. "It's a name I share with another person on this ship, and that counts for more than this."

Neptune remained with his arms by his sides, muscles tensed, as if ready for a fight. His black brows were low over his eyes and his jawline was rigid. His tawny skin glowed against his captain's uniform and I wondered about him, about the rumors I'd heard about his reputation, about him losing everything after he'd had an affair with a student at Space Academy.

My brain sorted through the intel I'd read in the file he deleted, about his days as a bounty hunter. I thought about his loner lifestyle and his need to keep me under his thumb. I felt a numbness in my chest that approached paralytic.

"Stryker," he said, his voice low and gravelly. "Don't leave."

"I have to leave. There's a real threat on this ship and somebody has to do something about it. I might not be as experienced as you or as strong as you, but I'm smart and determined and I won't let Faarstar take the lives of six crew members and almost fifty Gremlons."

I stormed out of Neptune's quarters. Right into the arms of a grey alien who'd been waiting in the hallway outside.

31: OMICRON FAARSTAR

Grey Four clamped his long, skinny hand over my face, covering my eyes, nose, and mouth. He wrapped his other arm around me, pinning my arms to my sides, and dragged me down the hallway, away from Neptune's room. If this had been a regular Moon Unit, there would have been passengers or crew or somebody to see me being dragged off. But it wasn't, and my chances of being seen were nil.

I tried to kick, struggle, slip out from under his arms, or otherwise get free. Greys had disproportionately long arms and wide, flat hands, and he'd placed both in a manner that restricted my most immediate needs. I wasn't going to get loose. I conserved my energy and waited for the next opportunity.

We reached the crew elevator and Grey Four pulled me inside. Immediately I smelled a foul odor. It was the dirty scent of an unwashed space pirate.

"Hello, Sylvia," said a playful voice. I recognized it as the same voice that had called out to me in engineering the day I'd first seen the greys.

I felt fingers on my hair. I pulled away. The voice laughed. "Let her breathe. She's no good to us dead."

Grey Four's fingers shifted, and my mouth was free. My instinct was to bite but I didn't yet know who or what this was about, and I thought it better to see my enemy before establishing a plan. "Who are you?" I said.

"The direct approach," he said. "Your father was the same way. Perhaps he'll have the chance to tell you about me." The fingers stroked my hair again. "Perhaps not."

If I'd felt paralytic in Neptune's quarters, then I felt dead inside now. "Omicron Faarstar," I said.

"You've heard of me? I'm flattered."

I turned to face him. The renditions and descriptions I'd heard about him from people who claimed to have seen him themselves had been far too complimentary. It was Omicron Faarstar in the flesh, though his gaunt appearance made "flesh" seem a generous descriptor.

His hair hung in clumps around his face, long and knotted and caked with unidentifiable grime. Hollow cheeks and dark undereye circles created visual holes in a skeleton-like face. His skin was papery, crinkled with the effects of too many atmospheres and too many climates. Yet his power was such that none of his hideousness mattered. He was respected, feared, admired, and served. By willing armies and kept slaves alike.

"If you heard what I heard, flattery wouldn't be the word that springs to mind."

He slapped me. The force was hard enough to knock me down. Grey Four let go. I landed on the floor of the elevator with my hands out to break my fall. I raised my hand to my cheek and slowly stood up to face the man who struck me.

"I won't let you destroy this ship," I said.

"Why would I destroy a ship? I'd be happy to add a Moon Unit to my fleet. Now the crew and passengers *on board* the Moon Unit, they're expendable."

"I won't let you murder the crew and the Gremlons on board," I said.

"You are a fighter, aren't you? It's a shame you never worked for me. I would have loved to have someone so feisty in my stable." He grinned, showing off jagged brown teeth from between chapped lips. "Frankly, your crew is a joke and the Gremlons are worthless. But you come with a high value. The daughter of turncoat Jack Stryker. Yes, I do believe you made this trip worth it, even if it did cost me the life of my courier."

"Mattix Dusk didn't work for you."

"Not knowingly," he said. He laughed. "But when your livelihood depends on working for the highest bidder, you learn not to ask questions about your employer."

"You murdered an innocent man."

"He is one of many. You should be pleased, Sylvia. I

have different plans for you."

The elevator doors opened, and Grey Four pushed me out. He held my wrists behind me in one of his hands. I stumbled forward. Faarstar stayed by my side, his putrid scent curling up my nose and into the back of my throat, turning my stomach.

"I'd love to make you more comfortable, but the luxury lodgings are currently occupied," he said to me. "Put her in the fuel cell," he said to the alien. Grey Four pushed me toward a nondescript door along the side of engineering.

Engineering. Which was empty now that Rune had left.

Engineering. Where I'd seen two greys talking before attempting to kill me and getting stunned by Neptune.

Engineering. Where the signal had originated that told us about the turbulence, the damage to the ship, and the advice to go into warp drive. The advice that would have destroyed us a billion miles ago had we course-corrected to avoid the made-up collision.

How long had Faarstar been on the ship? Long enough to set up camp on a relatively unattended floor.

With Rebel Rune off the ship, Faarstar would have had the run of the place. Did that confirm Rune's involvement or his fear? Faarstar would have needed an ally, and the engineer's unannounced getaway in the middle of the night spoke volumes about his willingness to only save himself. Highly recommended? That was a joke. Rebel Rune wasn't Space Academy material.

Grey Four pushed me into the fuel compartment and pulled the door shut behind me. Faarstar pressed a series of buttons outside the wall and bright red lights went on throughout the entire engineering sector. It altered the colors around me, making the grey all but disappear against the background.

I'd experienced this once before. Red lights in engineering indicated a gas leak. Quarantine. The color washed over the room, making all colors indistinguishable with my eyes. Faarstar said something to the grey, who nodded and took up a sentry position behind the navigational computer. Faarstar left.

There were two people on this ship who knew about Faarstar and one of us was helpless. If the ship crashed into Saturn at this point, I'd be the only one who would die knowing the truth. The other members of the crew would die thinking it was my fault.

I leaned against the back wall of the fuel cell. It was the Moon Unit equivalent of solitary confinement. Me, the fuel rods and power core, and a length of carpet that could have been white, gray, yellow, or red—all of which looked the same under the red lights.

The comm device in my ear was silent. If Neptune had been listening in, he'd know what happened. But my accusations about him had left little room for interpretation. If I'd been wrong, then he'd know his priority was saving the others. Not me. I could be sacrificed.

I knew Neptune would think that way because I'd stolen his lecture notes from the class he was supposed to teach. It wasn't until later that I'd learned that Neptune was the hot-shot guest lecturer, or that he'd been pulled from the course assignment because his demons had caught up with him. After Moon Unit 6, after reading the notes Neptune deleted the next day, I spent an afternoon snooping around his property. I found his lecture notes.

I saw what he'd wanted us to learn: you function as a team until the safety of the group can be guaranteed by the sacrifice of one member. It was a revolutionary concept that hadn't been taught in our 101 courses. Until that moment, I'd been led to believe your team was one unit. You survived or died together.

But that's not what Neptune believed. Talk about teachable moments. I was living his lesson plan even after removing myself from his tutelage.

Movement in engineering caught my eye. I shifted my position and looked out. Grey Four was entering coordinates into the computer. I had to squint to make out details. I slowly reclined and peered past the grey's legs for evidence that I wasn't going crazy.

I wasn't going crazy. Help had arrived. Unexpected, inconsequential, less-than-a-foot-tall help in the ridiculous package of a small, white, robot cat. Cat rolled across the carpet by the perimeter of the room and faced me. His eyes blinked twice. He spun and faced the grey, raised a paw, and fired.

Grey Four slunk down to the floor. Neptune rounded the corner and nudged the grey with the toe of his boot. The alien disintegrated into the carpet behind the desk.

32: NEPTUNE IN OPPOSITION

Neptune vacuumed Grey Four's remains with his space gun. I stood and slapped my hand on the inside of the fuel cell. Neptune picked up Cat and carried him to the wall. Cat raised his paw and fried the door activation panel. The door opened, and I rushed out.

"Don't say anything," Neptune commanded. "Your dad is on the bridge. I suggest you talk to him."

"Where are you going?"

"To find Faarstar."

Neptune was halfway to the door when I called out to him. "Thank you."

He turned back. "You're worth more to me alive than dead. That's all this is."

If ever there was a time to push emotions out of the way and act like the half Plunian I was, this was it. But I couldn't. I didn't want to deny that I had emotions or that I was more than a bargaining chip. It took everything I had to keep myself in check. By the time I reached the bridge, I was in emotional lockdown.

My dad wasn't alone. Ivi was at the communication board. Her face showed concern. I nodded once in greeting. My dad grabbed my arm and maneuvered me off the bridge. "Lieutenant Ivi, the bridge is in your hands."

"Yes, Commander."

My dad guided me to Council Chambers. When the doors shut behind us, he turned me toward him. "How much do you know?" he demanded.

His greeting wasn't what I expected from our first actual private conversation since learning he wasn't guilty, and I snapped. "That's it? No hello? No hi, daughter, we should catch up on what your life's been like since I was arrested? No small talk about dry ice mining? I mean, that's what you were, right? A dry ice miner?"

"My work delivering dry ice throughout the galaxy put me in a unique position. I was approached by Federation Council to work with them to infiltrate a pirate network. When I was arrested, it was because not arresting me would have meant certain death to you and your mother."

I shook my head, trying to make the thoughts make sense. "No," I said, not able to disengage from what I'd believed my whole life. "We're dry ice miners. You colluded with Cheung Qidd. You're the reason we don't have a planet anymore."

"I know what you thought. Telling you the truth

would have put you in danger."

"Did mom know?" I asked, shocked.

"Your mother always knew what I was doing."

He stared at me, his green eyes bright against his purple skin. Even though more than one source had told me he was innocent, I wanted to hate him for everything I'd lost. I wanted to have a person to blame. But he was too much like me. In color, in spirit, in determination. And if there was a modicum of truth to what he said, I wanted to hear it and believe even more than I wanted to hate.

"But you've been in jail for most of my life. When were they going to let you go?"

"I don't know. Somewhere in the council, someone thought it was better to let my cover story become the truth."

"How did you finally convince them to release you?"

"There was no benefit to holding me after Plunia was destroyed." He reached out and took my hand. "Faarstar isn't the only space pirate," he said. "There are entire networks in the galaxy. He's the most prominent because he likes the limelight. He's a dangerous man and he controls entire species. And he knows I'm the one who ultimately brought about Cheung Qidd's incarceration, and Qidd's network is the one Faarstar now controls."

"He destroyed everything we knew," I said quietly.

"Because of me. You were not wrong about that."

"And me? Why does he want me?"

"I have enemies, Sylvia. It's why Federation Council took me under their protection."

"Protection? You were arrested!"

"We had to make it look believable. I thought it would alienate you and your mother from dangers and allow you to live a safe life."

"And now? I know the risks of chip removal."

"I've survived the critical stage. It's too soon to tell if there will be long term damage. Doc acted in the way he thought was right. I cannot fault him for that."

I didn't know what to say. My entire belief system disintegrated under my feet like a dead grey alien. I didn't know what was true and what was a lie. First Neptune's betrayal, now this man in front of me who might as well have been a stranger. Our lives changed forever by his actions. To hear him speak rationally about his circumstances was a joke.

But I was on a spaceship where a crazy, megalomaniacal space pirate wanted me as a concubine. I wasn't exactly in a position to argue about stuff I couldn't change.

"Why did you come to the bridge?" he asked.

"Faarstar is on the ship. He has grey aliens working with him."

"How many?"

"I've seen three, but I can confirm two are dead. Either that's all there were or there are more, and if there are more, then we have no way of knowing where they are or how they got here."

"We?"

"Neptune and me."

"You and he work well together," he noted.

"Neptune's interest in me is avaricious." I felt a flush climb my face. "I think he's willing to use me to broker a deal with Faarstar to save the rest of the ship."

Unlike most of the unreadable expressions of Neptune, the one on my dad's face was plain as day. I knew we all had to work together if any of us were to survive, but professional partnerships didn't have to translate to friendship.

"Did you and he...?"

"That's none of your business."

"I need to know if I can trust him. The answer to my question is one component of the many facts that will help me make a determination."

I thought about everything I'd been through with Neptune. "He has extreme focus and will do whatever is required of him."

"Can *you* trust Neptune?" he asked.

"I don't think I have much of a choice."

33: BAD ROBOT

I spent the next half hour bringing my dad up to speed on our quickly multiplying issues. Pirates. Gremlons. Crew. Robots. Greys. All things led to one unavoidable conclusion: our only chance for survival was to act like a crew and get to Saturn.

I advised my dad to go to the uniform ward and outfit himself. I stayed in the privacy of Council Chambers. I didn't expect anyone to come looking for me there and I needed a quiet place to sort through everything we'd discussed.

We already knew Doc had contacted Federation Council about an escaped convict on board the ship. Representatives from the council would be waiting for our arrival, along with military police and guards. Whether they'd take my dad back into custody for show or for real didn't matter. It was simply a fact in our formulating plan, a variable that meant Saturn held a slight edge as our destination because on Saturn, we'd essentially have backup.

Other variables were less easy to quantify. Gremlons couldn't be counted on to fight and might represent more of a distraction than a help. Just because they were our most numerous allies didn't mean they weren't safer in Ion-54. The crew, well, I didn't know. Rune had made his intentions clear when he stole the escape pod. His actions had made it so nobody else on the ship could escape. There would be no future for Rebel Rune with the Moon Unit Corporation if any of us survived and could report him. Maybe that had been part of his considerations. If we all died, nobody would know.

Rune's absence didn't automatically remove suspicion from the others on board. T-Fal had been with Pika when she recorded the message, and T-Fal belonged to Kentaro. What did the medic have to do with any of this?

Ivi was the only other woman on the ship. Was she my ally? Were we bound by the battle of the sexes? Or were her alliances with her Martian species, a species that had shown considerable distaste for Plunians ever since I'd first met them?

And there was the troubling matter of what Mattix had been couriering. Faarstar said Mattix worked for the highest bidder. I knew this to be somewhat true. Couriers had dangerous jobs and took lots of risks. The pay was commensurate with the job. It explained why Mattix knew how to defend himself. Hapkido was great for hand to hand combat, but it wouldn't do much against a space gun or vaporizer.

Even my assertation that we could trust Neptune came with a side of doubt. I felt more confident trusting in Cat, who had taken out Grey Four in engineering, than the acting captain of the ship.

Wait a minute.

I'd never programmed Cat with lasers that could kill. He'd been my companion and my pet. A robot computer who understood commands and recorded data and reacted to light with a wake-up meow and sometimes even purred on command. He'd gone to Saturn with Pika where she'd recorded a message to send back to me. But Pika wouldn't know the first thing about death rays. Neptune would.

Neptune. Who I already knew had tampered with Cat. Neptune, who complained about using a male pronoun for a robot cat. Neptune would never have gotten into the habit of using that pronoun if he hadn't spent a fair amount of time with the robot cat in question. And Neptune knew all about death rays and lasers and programming computers.

I left Council Chambers. T-Fal was in the hallway. He followed me down the hall to Neptune's quarters. I now understood why Neptune had moved my stuff to his room. It was another way to keep an eye on me. How long had he known how this trip would go? He'd been the one to arrange my dad's presence on the ship. Had it been his endgame all along? It sickened me to have to go in and face him.

I reached out for the door open panel. The doors swished apart before I made contact. I braced myself in case Neptune was inside and T-Fal rolled into me.

"Not now, T-Fal," I said. "Go to Medi-Bay."

"Lieutenant Stryker, I have been programmed to follow you."

"By who? Kentaro?"

"No, Lieutenant Stryker. By Captain Neptune."

Enough was enough.

There'd been a time when I thought Neptune's attention toward me had been charming. Maybe I even liked it a little. After the heartbreak caused when Vaan Marshall chose politics (and a seat on Federation Council) over me, I'd viewed romantic entanglements as a nuisance. And I'd pretty much succeeded until I got a job with Moon Unit Corp and met Neptune. The pull I felt toward him was different. And because he'd met me under completely separate circumstances than my ostracized life on Plunia, I'd allowed myself to enjoy it.

But now, with the benefit of clarity, I wanted to go back to being invisible. Like the days when everybody looked the other way when I entered a room. The stores that pretended not to see me standing in line waiting to place an order. There was a comfort in anonymity. Being purple was a big enough strike against me in that category. But being followed by a robot programmed to trail me was too freaking much.

Except, thanks to Yoka, I knew how to go into Neptune's room and remain invisible.

"T-Fal, can you enter Neptune's quarters?"

"Yes, Lieutenant Stryker. I have been programmed to bypass the security measures on all doors of the Moon Unit Mini 7.2."

"Perfect." I dropped down to my hands and knees and wrapped my arms around T-Fal's cylindrical base to find a way to open his hidden compartment. I turned my head to the side and felt the cold metal pressed against my cheek. It had been so easy for Yoka. Why couldn't I figure it out?

"Stryker," Neptune said. I turned my head and looked up. He was in his trademark stance. I, sadly, was on my knees with my arms wrapped around the bottom half of a robot. The definition of compromising position. And it was at that point that my fingers found the release button and the hidden compartment on T-Fal opened up.

And exposed Pika, the scared, pink alien we'd been going to so much trouble to rescue.

34: INNOCENCE FOUND

I'd never seen Pika so small. She wore the special courier uniform I made for her before she left with Mattix, but it was so big on her it looked like a dirty silver potato sack. She was pressed against the back of the compartment with her arms wrapped around her bent legs. Knobby knees protruding up, her face hidden mostly behind them. Her eyes were wide, and her ears were flat against her head.

"Open the door," I said to Neptune. I kept my eyes on Pika.

Neptune held his hand out and the doors opened. "T-Fal, follow Neptune."

The large robot glided into the room. I slipped inside before the doors closed. I reached my hands into the compartment and pulled out Pika. She jumped up and threw her skinny pink arms around my neck and wrapped her legs around my waist and smothered me with kisses.

For a moment, I couldn't breathe.

"Pika!"

She hopped down. "Are you mad mad mad?"

Mad? That was one word for it. "How long have you been on the ship?"

"The whole time you were on the ship."

"No. That's not possible."

"Yes, it is. I hid in the giant's suitcase." She bent her head down and then peeked up at me from under long eyelashes. "But it's okay. He knew." Her ears twitched, and she blinked a couple of times. I wanted to be mad at her but couldn't. I turned to Neptune, who I had more than enough anger for.

"You knew?" I said. He didn't respond. "Do you realize what this means? We're on a rescue mission for someone who doesn't need to be rescued. Unless this was your plan all along?" Walls of reality closed in on me like a trash compactor. "You orchestrated this entire thing to get me to Saturn. This had nothing to do with saving Pika. You used her. You're using all of us. I suspected there was someone working on the inside, but not you. I never suspected you."

He kept his eyes on me but addressed Pika. "Pika, I need you to get back inside T-Fal and go to Ion-54. Stay with the other Gremlons."

"No," she said. "I want to play with Sylvia."

"I need to talk to Lieutenant Stryker. Alone."

"No no no," she said quietly.

I looked at Pika. She was from the most taken-advantage of species in the galaxy and she was standing up to Neptune to show me support.

"Thank you, Pika," I said, "but I promised the Gremlons some freeze-dried ice cream and I bet they'd like it if you brought it to them." I dumped the contents of my suitcase into a bag. "Neptune and I have some things to say to each other and I don't think you should hear them."

Her eyes got wide and her pupils dilated. She looked at Neptune. "Are you finally going to tell her?"

"Tell me what?" I demanded.

"The truth!" She dropped my hand and clapped hers and then hopped from one foot to the other like she had to go to the bathroom.

"I already know the truth," I said.

"No, you don't don't don't," Pika said.

"Yes, I do."

"No," Neptune said, "You don't." He turned to Pika. "If you want a place to live when we get back from Saturn, you need to leave this room now."

"Okay okay okay!" she said. Her grin was wide enough to show off her fifty small pointy teeth. She dropped to the floor and crawled back inside T-Fal. The hidden compartment slid into place and the robot spun 180 degrees.

"Take cargo to Ion-54," Neptune said. "Protect her at all costs."

"Yes, Captain." T-Fal rolled toward the door.

From the bottom of T-Fal, I heard Pika's soft, high voice. "La la la la la."

Neptune pounded the outside of the robot with his closed fist. "No singing."

"Okay okay okay."

When the doors were closed, Neptune spoke. "Sit down, Stryker."

"I'll stand."

"That was an order."

"You're not my captain, you're my capt*or*. You tricked me into this whole trip. I hope they're making it worth your while."

This time Neptune stepped closer. I stepped back. He kept advancing until my back was against the wall and he was right in front of me.

He put his hands on the wall on either side of my head and leaned in. "You don't know how wrong you are," he said. His eyes flashed black. "This trip was never about financial gain. What I want from you has nothing to do with collecting a bounty. I thought you knew that by now."

I flushed from the closeness of him. "Whatever you're hiding, whatever it is you don't want me to know about you, just tell me."

"It's not about me. It's about you."

"How are you going to tell me about my personal history? What could you possibly think I don't already know?"

"You don't know the truth about why your records at Space Academy were sealed." His eyes never left my face. I was aware of the heat between us, like electrically charged atoms had been released, making my skin prickle. "It had nothing to do with the timing of your father's arrest or the fake charges of collusion with Cheung Qidd. You acted out, and the academy had no choice but to take disciplinary action. But you were never expelled. That's why they sealed your files."

"That doesn't make sense. I got into fights, and one of those fights led to the death of a Martian student. It's the reason I continue to have trouble with Martians and the reason I don't know if I can trust Ivi."

Neptune turned away and unlocked a trunk that sat on his table. Inside was a flat disc. He inserted the disc into a small, black handheld media player, flipped the top open, and handed the device to me.

The screen was black and white and poorly rendered but I recognized the Space Academy insignia at the top. Below was a letter signed by the academy president, followed by his thumbprint next to his signature.

None of that was as interesting as the content of the letter that confirmed what Neptune was trying to say.

35: THE LIES WE LEARN TO BELIEVE

I dropped onto the corner of Neptune's bed and read the document. Twice. I looked up at Neptune. "These documents say I was granted leave from my education and should I return, the costs of my schooling were to be covered by the Federation Council."

"Yes."

"Why would they do that?"

"The same reason they offered you the Plunian relief fund after your planet was destroyed. You showed great potential."

"I was just a student."

"You were one of the brightest brains to come through the academy in a long time. People were watching you."

"And then my dad got arrested and I acted up and that was it." I waved the computer. "Except it wasn't it. But nobody told me. Why didn't anybody tell me?"

"There have been rumors of corruption in Federation Council for years. When your dad went into protective custody, the operation he was involved in halted. He was too much a part of the fight against the pirates to use as bait to flush out the corruption, so his incarceration became a fact. The risks of indicating to the galaxy that he was anything other than a prisoner were too great."

"And what about me? While Federation Council investigated my dad, they took ownership of the mines and kept my mom on in a barely paid role. I left school and helped because she couldn't afford to hire anybody."

"Yes. And a lot of people kept their eyes on you. Had you been anything other than what you said you were, you would have been picked up too. But you weren't. You gave up everything you had been taught and joined the family business."

"A business nobody wanted to support."

"You taught yourself on the side. You made yourself invaluable to people who would have shunned you. And slowly the customers returned."

"How do you even know this?" I asked, waving the handheld device around.

"I pulled your file."

"When?"

"After you pulled mine."

So he knew.

Learning about Neptune's side job collecting bounties was only one of the things I'd discovered in his file. He'd been a mystery to me after that first Moon Unit 5 trek. His actions had been more by-the-book than I'd ever witnessed before. He followed the BOP, he recognized rank, and he did his job, even when the price had been higher than I'd ever seen a person pay. I'd hacked my way onto that ship to act as the uniform lieutenant and had finished it with a greater education than I'd gotten in advanced level courses.

In the break between Moon Treks, I'd gotten Zeke to help me access classified content by hacking our way behind the firewall at the Federation Council library and accessing documents we shouldn't have been able to see. It started out as a side project. Learn about the space pirate who had destroyed my planet.

Cheung Qidd had been incarcerated for 71,187 days and had remained silent for 71,186 of them. The transcripts from when he finally broke his pirate code made for weeks of reading during the day and under the covers of my thermal blanket at night. Two names had shown up repeatedly: Jack Stryker, and Neptune. It was the appearance of Neptune's name in those transcripts that first made me suspect he knew more than he said, and he'd gone to great lengths to keep me from finding out what that was.

Zeke, uninterested in my burgeoning obsession, spent that time hauling moon rocks from the local crater to the yard behind his dad's house. I read. Three thousand, two hundred, and twenty-seven pages. And even though Zeke and I had accessed the content from behind firewalls more secure than the protective atmospheric barriers on formerly unlivable planets, enough of the information had been redacted to leave me with questions about my dad.

But not about Neptune.

Omicron Faarstar had implicated Neptune in a military assignment that I'd never heard about. The operation had crippled Faarstar's army and freed an entire colony of prisoners and slaves. It had undermined the existing fear that allowed space pirates to get away with as much as they did.

After that operation, families were united. Alliances were formed. Residents fought back. Some said it was a turning point. Others said it had led to corruption on a smaller scale. The only thing the powers that be agreed upon was that Neptune receive no public praise for leading the operation. Privately, he'd been awarded the highest recognition possible. A single star embossed on the back of his dog tags.

That's how I knew where he kept his dog tags. I needed to see for myself.

Pika had caught me. That's why she sewed them into the hem of my thermal sleepwear. She knew Neptune considered them valuable. To her they were merely shiny. But I was her friend and she liked to give her friends presents—whether those presents were hers to give or not. I snuck the dog tags back to Neptune's room and kept my knowledge of his secrets to myself.

And my fear of being used, my lingering sense that I was worthless as anything other than a bargaining chip, had allowed me to believe the worst about Neptune. Not the best.

I set the small black document viewer on the bed and stared at a spot of nothing across the room. The evidence that my whole life hadn't been what I thought was right there, but that didn't make it any easier to swallow. It was like someone told me I was orange. Just saying so wouldn't make me see my reflection as anything other than purple.

"I don't know what I'm supposed to do with this information," I said, my eyes fixed on the wall.

"That's up to you," Neptune said. "But there's a threat on this ship, and I can use your help. I'll be on the bridge. When you make your decision, report." He left.

My very personal struggle and the very real threat on the ship were too much. And hearing the truth from Neptune, him delivering the news with military precision, was both the best and worst way to have learned. If what he'd said was true, then I could still go on to have everything I'd ever wanted.

But were those arrangements a form of hush money? If I accepted them, would I be owned and controlled by the Federation Council? The price felt too high.

I wanted to shed my skin and start over. I did the next best thing. I took off my uniform and boots and stepped into the deionization chamber. The BOP recommended purification showers last a minimum of 2.7 minutes long, enough to dissolve space debris and possible contaminants. The timer went off, but I didn't move. I let the sanitizing ions pelt me long after my time was up. I rested my arms against the wall in front of me and leaned my head on them and waited for tears that never came. I was so lost in my self-pity that I didn't notice the deionization chamber switch off right away. When I did, I knew I wasn't alone.

36: VULNERABLE

Being naked, alone, and emotionally vulnerable on a spaceship where a diabolical pirate with a vendetta against my family was roaming free was disconcerting enough but judging from the hum throughout my body and the subtle glow that radiated from my skin, I knew without turning around that Neptune was back. It figured this time I was naked. But the information Neptune had given me exposed more than my uniform usually kept hidden, and he'd known it first. I would not be embarrassed by this moment. It was what it was.

I kept my back to him but stood up straight. He could do whatever it was he'd returned to the room to do and leave.

I didn't hear him leave.

He unlatched the door to the deionization chamber and stepped in behind me. And then, I felt a garment drop onto my shoulders. I looked down. It was Neptune's captain uniform jacket. He put his hands on my arms on top of the fabric and leaned in close to my ear. "Stryker," he said. "What I told you doesn't change anything. You're still you."

The exhaustion from everything that had happened since I'd first seen the recording that Pika had programmed into Cat, coupled with the unexpected news and the ion shower, wiped me out. I didn't want to think about any of it. I leaned back against Neptune and closed my eyes. He wrapped his arms around me. The clean, fresh, oxygenated air and the subtle sanitizing odor that lingered mixed with Neptune's scent: moon dust and fresh figs.

I couldn't remember the last time someone had held me to provide comfort and not to teach me how to break from a defensive hold. I was thankful that I'd never turned around because Neptune's gesture aroused emotions that I wouldn't have been able to hide. I put my hands on his forearms and didn't say a word.

In the middle of a galaxy of capitalistic moon travel tourist businesses, space pirates who treated lives as commodities, corrupt officials in the governing federation bodies, and malfunctioning robots, what I felt for Neptune was real. There were a hundred reasons why it would never amount to more than us working side by side on a mission, but I knew it wasn't a figment of my imagination. And after being as alone as someone could be, having an unspoken bond was priceless.

I slipped my arms into the sleeves of Neptune's jacket and buttoned it. When I turned to face him, I noticed his dog tags on a chain around his neck, resting against his simple white cotton T-shirt.

"Lieutenant Stryker reporting for duty," I said quietly.

He put his hand under my chin and stared into my eyes. I already knew he wouldn't ask if I was sure. That wasn't how he was trained.

"Someone on this ship is working for Faarstar," he said. "Until we determine who that is, we have to treat all crew members as if it could be them."

"Can we reach Saturn without relying on the crew?"

"Yes. I leaked to the crew that new navigational charts have been entered into the computer. Anybody who tries to access them or see where we're headed will think we're planning to circle Saturn and return to the base. If they try to override those directions, I'll get a ping."

"But Rune wiped out the charts. The only way to get to Saturn is to have a pilot fly us there. That's why we need my dad."

"No mission is without risks."

Neptune bent his head down and gently pressed his lips against mine. The kiss was soft and tender and more satisfying than fresh Plunian ice cream whipped with an oxygen charge. An internal tingling sensation flooded through my arms and legs. He pulled away and held my face in his hands, brushing my lips with his thumb. I didn't want to move.

"There's this thing I have to do," he said. He stepped back and smiled, and then turned away and headed toward the door.

I eased his jacket off. "Neptune," I said to his back. "You can't go to the bridge without your uniform."

He turned back. I held the crisp white jacket at arm's length. Neptune's dark eyes scanned me slowly from face to feet and back to my face. He returned, his eyes never leaving mine.

He took the jacket from my hand. My purple nakedness was electric. Hey, if we were all about to die, none of this mattered, right? And we were in the captain's quarters. Nobody was going to find out what we did if neither of us told, and I'd recently learned Neptune knew how to keep a secret.

He eased his jacket on and bent his head down to my ear. "You're vulnerable," he said. "I won't take advantage of that. But don't mistake that for me not wanting more." He slipped the chain with his dog tags over his head and transferred it to my neck. The metal was cool against my flushed lavender flesh. I closed my hand around the tags.

He retrieved my uniform from the floor and handed it to me. I held it up in a poor excuse for modesty. He pulled his jacket on slowly, never breaking eye contact.

My emotions churned. Rational and irrational thoughts swirled together, meshed and merged, collided and clashed.

I put my hand on his wrist to keep him from leaving. I wanted this moment to last forever. I closed my eyes and breathed in the lingering scent of him. A quiet whirring sound came from the other side of the door and then the doors slid open. T-Fal stood in the hallway.

"Captain Neptune," he said. "You have a visitor."

Neptune dropped his hands and turned to face the door. T-Fal rolled in and revealed the one person who had no business walking in on Neptune and me in our states of dress/undress.

We'd just been caught by my dad.

37: CAUGHT IN THE ACT

While I had no idea what brought my dad to Neptune's quarters, it seemed apparent that the last thing he'd expected to walk in on was a sexually charged moment. Especially considering the last conversation we'd had was about Neptune's plans to turn me over to Faarstar. While he'd been getting into uniform, I'd been getting out of mine.

Everything that had happened since our talk had left me with a shifted sense of loyalty, but to my dad, it probably looked like I was being played. A poor little girl with romantic notions being hoodwinked by an intergalactic bad boy. And while I saw myself as neither poor nor little, I recognized the look in Jack Stryker's eyes and it was not understanding.

Aside from the uniform I held in front of my body, I was naked, but I did nothing more to cover myself. Neptune stood in front of me to block my dad's view (at least I thought that was why he stood there).

"Jack," he said. "This isn't—" he turned his head and looked at me.

This isn't what? This isn't what it looks like? It kind of was. This isn't the time for a surprise visit? I agreed. This isn't your business? That was for darn sure. But I never got to hear what he was about to say because my dad interrupted him.

"The scanners have identified a rapidly approaching cluster of spaceships. It's too soon to tell if they're under pirate rule or otherwise. We've entered unrestricted airspace, and this may be the first of many curiosity seekers."

"Wait for me on the bridge," Neptune said. The two men glared at each other and then the one related to me left.

While Neptune's back was to me, I stepped into my uniform and pulled it on. I raised the zipper and grabbed my tights from a separate pile on the floor. Neptune swiftly buttoned his jacket and addressed T-Fal. "Identify who uploaded authorization codes for you to access my quarters."

T-Fal's spinner rotated a few times and buttons on his front panel lit. Seconds later, he spoke. "Captain's quarters access code program written by Lieutenant Sylvia Stryker."

Neptune turned to me. I stood on one foot, with the other foot raised and my tights in my hand. "What?" I said. "You told me these were my quarters too. I figured it was the one place nobody would look for me."

"Pack up your things when you're dressed. You're getting your own quarters until we reach Saturn."

Neptune left. I fingered his dog tags and then slipped them inside the collar of my uniform. They dangled between my breasts, an unexpectedly intimate feeling that would interfere with my focus and concentration. I pulled on my boots and carried all my things to the uniform ward.

Neptune had his mission: Get us safely to Saturn. My dad had his mission: arrest or kill Omicron Faarstar. Both were important. Both would require all our attention. But neither took into consideration that Mattix Dusk had been killed and unless I found out why, his killer would go free.

Which meant I had my mission too. Identify Mattix's killer and bring him or her to justice.

I still didn't know who was working with Faarstar. T-Fal's presence when Pika made the recording put him at the scene and that led me to believe Kentaro wasn't without suspicion. However, Kentaro was a medic. And if Mattix had requested help, a medic would have replied. Logically, T-Fal would have been with him. So while I couldn't ignore that Kentaro had opportunity, he was the one person on the ship who'd had a legitimate reason for being there.

I couldn't say the same thing for the others who had answered my last-minute employment call.

After securing Neptune's dog tags to the inside of my uniform with High Durability Tape, I signed into the computer and accessed the Moon Unit Corp private messaging boards. It felt like far more than three days had passed since I placed the ad for crew members. I paged backward through the messages to identify the open job post I had left and looked at the applications of those who'd applied.

"Computer, show me Lieutenant Ivi's application and medical file."

A file folder labeled with the Martian's name appeared on the screen. I tapped the icon and the file opened. First thing I checked was the application. It was filled out in full and nothing unusual stood out. I moved on to her background check and confirmed the details T-Fal had dictated in Council Chambers. Fluent in over four hundred languages. Experience in charting map coordinates. Trained in several fighting styles. Nothing about the application or background indicated anything other than what she appeared to be.

"Computer, show me Kentaro's application and medical file."

A second file folder appeared on the screen. I tapped the icon and scanned his application and then his background check. Like T-Fal had told us, Kentaro was ex-military. Suffered a crippling leg wound in battle and was forced to leave his position. T-Fal had told us that there were no records on Kentaro for the past twenty years, but Kentaro himself had explained that away. I studied the background check from the Moon Unit computer to see how well it matched up with what Kentaro had told us.

I wasn't surprised to find the discrepancy.

Medic Kentaro had indeed fought in the war between Mars and Venus. And he had also been injured to the point of not being able to fight. What he hadn't disclosed that the computer now did was that the injury wasn't sustained in battle. It was the result of a fight with his captain in a neutral bar on Colony 5. Instead of receiving immediate treatment that would have saved his limb, his squadron was called to action and left him behind.

As a medic, he could have used his cauterizing ray to prevent infection, seal the wound, and request transport to a local medical facility. He hadn't. He drank away the pain with bootleg booze and passed out.

He was found the next morning, infected with an alien virus that caused chronic pain and inflammation. At the time of the war, the contaminant was a known pirate tactic. Inject injured soldiers. Offer treatment. Claim them as slaves.

There was no cure for the virus, and in Kentaro's case, the leg had to be amputated. The only viable treatment was to manage the pain with medication. And the pills, quickly regulated by opportunistic pharma suppliers, was most easily gotten through couriers who could hide their booty in cargo holds filled with more routine pickups.

More interesting than that was the name of the courier Kentaro relied on to supply the black-market medication needed to ease his pain.

Mattix Dusk.

38: NOT WHAT YOU THOUGHT

It was there in black and white. Kentaro's connection to Mattix. Why he'd have a reason to contact him, and, depending on his level of desperation, why he'd have a reason to kill him. The medic on board the ship would have needed a courier to supply him with pain medication, and Kentaro already told us he knew Mattix. I'd wanted to believe he was one of us, fighting against the villains we fought against, but leaving blinders on at this point was irresponsible.

I was about to radio the bridge but stopped. Anyone with a motive could listen in on that communication. I had to let Neptune know what I knew and there was one other way to do it.

"Neptune, it's Stryker."

Silence.

"Neptune. Listen to me. I found something in Kentaro's background check that none of us saw. Are you there?"

Silence.

"Come on! Forget about what I said about my comm device. This is about the mission. We're in danger. *You're* in danger. I think Kentaro is working for Faarstar. He has a grudge against my dad. He could have gotten the grey aliens on the ship, he could have messed with our coordinates, and he could have faked the turbulence. Where are you?"

Silence.

They say to be careful what you wish for and that couldn't have been truer than it was right now. I'd accepted Neptune's security measures of giving me a uniform with a communication chip on Moon Unit 5 and having a communicator inserted in my ear for Moon Unit 6. I knew from studying security measures that black ops equipment existed and hadn't thought twice about it until Neptune's motivations appeared more mercenary than military. I'd said it was creepy. I'd called him a stalker. And to show me how wrong I was, he'd turned the comm device off when I needed to communicate with him the most.

But doing my job wasn't about relying on shortcuts. This was critical intel and as a member of the crew, it was my job to get the intel to the captain.

I was halfway to the bridge when something slammed into the ship.

The impact knocked me off balance and I fell into the wall. My neck jerked with whiplash. A splitting headache from the jarring change in air pressure speared my temple. I kept both hands out, feeling for the railing, and sought footing.

A second hit knocked me off balance again. Whoever or whatever was attacking us was relentless. We were a small ship with a smaller crew. We couldn't sustain much more of this.

I stumbled forward. Twice I lost my balance. Twice I pulled myself back up and powered on. My dad had reported that a fleet of unidentifiable ships was approaching, and the attack revealed their mission: they intended to harm us. That was not good.

The bridge wasn't far, but it took ample time to reach it. When the doors slid open and I entered, I found Ivi at the communication computer. Neptune stood behind the captain's chair with his hands on the back of it. Another blast hit the ship and we all fell to the right.

This time I didn't stand up. "Who's attacking us?" I asked—a general question for either of them to answer.

Ivi replied first. "The ships are unmarked. There are four of them. I've opened a channel for communication, but no one has responded." She tipped her head to the side and touched the silver device in her ear. "Hello, I repeat, hello. This is Moon Unit Mini 7.2 requesting a visual. We are a cruise ship with passengers on our way to Saturn. We intend no harm."

We all watched her. After a few seconds, she shook her head. No answer.

"Captain Neptune," she said. "Have you considered opening a channel for those of us on the ship to contact our families?"

Ivi didn't spell out her reason for asking, but it was clear. She saw this ending one way. In our destruction. She wanted a chance to say goodbye. It was a touching request. And she hadn't asked it with malice or judgment or insubordination. There'd been no apology for thinking of herself and not the rest of us. Any captain in our situation would have approved her request.

I turned to look at the screen. Without accepting our request for a visual, the only thing we could go on was the image of the four ships heading our way. They were small and in tight formation. The only other time I'd seen spaceships fly that close together was an air show. It took a talented pilot to maneuver with such limited boundaries.

Something about the image didn't fit with the threats. A large asteroid flew in the path of the lead ship and it pulled down its nose to compensate. The remaining three ships all followed in perfect harmony. They bounded back up to their former flight angle and continued toward us. Everything I knew about space pirates and renegade spaceships that traveled unrestricted areas of the galaxy was that they were showoffs. Wild. Uncontrollable. They didn't pay attention to flight plans and neat formations. That's not who this was.

Ivi's question to Neptune hung unacknowledged and something about it struck me as off. Her request was standard, but only if she knew there was no chance of survival. And to her, to anybody on this ship except for Neptune and me, there *was* a chance of survival. It was stated in the BOP.

If a Moon Unit in flight sustains damage that threatens the lives of the passengers, emergency evacuation procedure dictates the captain and two officers of his choice stay with the ship while all others convene to the escape pod. Once deployed from the ship, LIDAR technology will activate and return the pod to the docking station of origination with no further action required by passengers.

That was it. If Ivi thought we were going to die, she would either ask Neptune which two crew members he directed to remain or when she could go to the escape pod. But she wasn't asking either of those questions. And there were only two people on this ship who had full knowledge that Rebel Rune had already taken off with the escape pod. Neptune and me.

I looked at Ivi. Her round green face was hopeful. If I were to judge her motivations strictly by her body language and her attitude, I'd state to any judge in the galaxy that she intended us no harm, but she feared for her safety.

Without realizing it, I held my hand palm-face out. "Hold on," I said. I turned toward the screen and watched the ships. "Open a new channel," I said.

"Captain?"

I felt Neptune watching me while I watched the

screen. The ships drew closer and stayed in perfect formation.

"Stryker, report."

"Emergency protocol dictates that non-essential crew head to the escape pod."

I didn't have to remind Neptune that we were a ship without an escape pod. The expression on his face, unreadable to probably anybody who hadn't made a careful study of the subtleties of his eyebrow movement, told me he already knew what I suspected.

He turned his back to me and addressed Ivi. "Lieutenant, have you received communication from the approaching series of ships?"

It was a direct question. Lying would be grounds for dismissal and indication of motivations that were not aligned with those of the ship. Judging from Ivi's silence, she was aware of all of that and was going to protect herself by not saying a word.

That didn't work for me.

"If you knew the ship was in trouble, you wouldn't have requested a channel to communicate with your family. You would have requested leave from your position to get to the escape pod. But you didn't. You already know there's no escape pod on this ship anymore, don't you?"

Her eyes widened, and she showed real fear. Not bravery, not animosity, not anger. Fear. I turned back to Neptune. "Those ships aren't the people attacking us. They're here to save us." I turned back to Ivi. "You know who's piloting those ships, don't you?"

She nodded. "He said he'd come back for us and he did." She pointed to the screen. "The pilot in front is Rebel Rune."

39: ASTRONOVAS

"When Rune took off in the middle of the night, we thought he was working with the space pirates," I said. "We thought he was the one giving Faarstar information on the ship and mucking around with the course charts."

Ivi removed the communication device from her ear and set it on the keyboard. "Request permission to speak freely, Captain."

Neptune pointed to the screen. "Make it fast. If he's not the one attacking us, then somebody else is."

"Rune is the founder of the AstroNovas. It's a flight demonstration squadron. He told me if he could get off the ship and back to the docking station, he could come back with help." She pointed to the screen. "That's help. Rune and three of his squadron members."

That's why the ships flew in such perfect harmony. They trained for maneuvers that stunned and delighted spectators. They represented a celebratory branch of the space military. Everything on Rune's application had been true. He'd just failed to mention the details.

"I believe you," I said. Neptune glared at me. "What? I'm trained to spot all fifty-seven verity tells in under thirty seconds. Martians are capable of a lot of things, but not lying on this level. She's telling the truth."

Unlike me. All along, Ivi had been what she seemed. So was Rune. Maybe they'd both been telling the truth, but much of what I'd said and done on this trek made me a liar.

"Lieutenant Ivi, open up a channel to Lieutenant Rune," Neptune said.

"Captain, with all due respect, he hasn't responded to our attempts to communicate so far. If the Moon Unit sustained damage to the identification triangulators, it's likely Rune can't determine where the communication request is coming from."

There was one direct line of communication that Rune could not reject or ignore, and it came from the captain's chair. For the first time since we'd departed, Neptune lowered himself into the one seat on the ship he seemed to think he wasn't qualified to occupy. He rested his hands on the arms and pressed a large, square, blue button. "Moon Unit to Rebel Rune. Requesting dialogue. Communications friendly. Over."

Rune's voice sounded over the speakers. "Lieutenant Rune reporting for rescue duty."

"Requesting visual."

"Visual granted."

The window that looked out over the vastness of space filled with a pop-up image. It showed the bridge of another ship and Rune as the pilot.

"We've been attacked," Neptune said. "The monitors are out of commission and we can't tell the extent of the damage. Engineering is, well, you're our engineer, and without you, we're in crisis management. Can you see who else is out here with us or provide any information?"

"Whoever was out here didn't want company," Rune said. "They scattered before we reached you and now it's just you and us. We'll do a ship scan to make sure you're okay to continue to Saturn." The four spaceships broke formation and flew at us. One went over us, two went on either side, and the last one flipped upside down and went below. Seconds later, they returned and regrouped. "There's no visual damage," Rune said. "Are you sure about your intel?"

Reality converged with Rune's report. "It was an attractor beam," I said. "We tried to use one in the dry ice mines on Plunia. It attracts one object to another through birefringent and light beam manipulation. I didn't know it could work on this magnitude, but we're in zero gravity so weight wouldn't be an issue."

"You say you tried to get them to work. What happened?"

"The heat from the light index melted the dry ice and wiped out our product yield. It was too risky to keep trying and failing so we abandoned the idea."

"Did you build it?"

"No. My dad did."

It made sense that my dad would have shared that information with Cheung Qidd while working undercover. To us on Plunia, the invention was a failure. It would have seemed a minor thing to give up to gain trust. But this was no dry ice field, and the principals of my dad's attractor beam could have been made to work on a much larger scale.

Neptune stood.

"Where are you going?" I asked.

"To talk to Jack."

"Our ship needs a captain. Let me handle this."

Neptune nodded once and handed me his space gun. I attached it to my belt and left.

The information I'd discovered about Kentaro remained unreported. As I made my way through the white hallways, I was aware that threats could come from just about anywhere. I rounded corner after corner, keeping one hand on the wall to steady myself in the event of another shake-up.

At the last curving hallway, I found an odd sight. T-Fal with his arm extended and Cat mounted on the end staring at him at eye level. The larger robot turned his head toward me.

I held my hands up. "T-Fal, this isn't the time to play. Take Cat back to my quarters. No, wait, I don't have quarters. Take Cat to the Gremlons and let them play with him, then meet me in security section."

"Program in progress," T-Fal said. He turned his head back toward Cat. Cat's eyes lit up and a beam of red light shot out at T-Fal. The robot's silver metal turned orange, glowing with heat. I ran forward and pulled Cat off T-Fal's arm.

It was too late. A coil broke loose and dangled out of T-Fal's neck and his lights turned off. Cat's emergency laser had fried the robot's panel and left him as little more than a pile of non-stick Teflon. Like most robots, he could be repaired, but for now the only thing T-Fal was good for was making breakfast.

Why had Cat fried T-Fal? Who had programmed that command?

I flipped Cat over and opened the panel that protected his main circuit board. I searched for signs he'd been tampered with. I was so absorbed that I didn't hear the elevator arrive.

"Sylvia." My dad stepped out of the unit, but stayed ten feet away from me, as if he wouldn't come closer until he knew I was okay with it.

"Dad," I said. The single syllable word was too much for me, and a volcano of emotions erupted.

He rushed forward and pulled me into a hug. He wasn't wired to comfort me or console me. He wasn't supposed to compensate for human emotions, even if they came from his half-human daughter. But he did, and I hugged him back.

"When we land on Saturn, is Federation Council going to take you away again?" I asked.

"No. I'll go into debriefing while they take Faarstar into custody."

"And then you'll be free?"

"The only way to secure my freedom was to deliver Faarstar and bring an end to the Qidd-Faarstar space pirate dynasty."

"That's what this was all about, wasn't it? I know you knew Neptune. I read transcripts of Qidd's statement. Neptune told me he was the one who brought you in, and I know he was the one who arrested Qidd. Now you're working together to bring down Faarstar. Neither of you wanted me to know."

"You always were smart, Sylvia." He smiled with barely concealed pride. "Neptune contacted me in prison and expedited my release so I could help him on your recent trip to Venus. I contacted him with this mission. I didn't know you two had a—I didn't know about your relationship. I might have rethought my decision if I did."

"Your decision was sound."

"Be that as it may, we're here. I told him to procure a ship and I would be on board. Your presence surprised me as much as my presence surprised you."

I didn't tell my dad that his presence hadn't been a surprise because Neptune had told me. Neptune's loyalty had been to me, not Jack Stryker. And now I understood why Neptune knew Moon Unit Corporation wasn't looking for us, why he was finishing what he'd started, and why there'd been so much effort put into keeping secrets from me.

There was one more thing that I needed to know. "Dad, what happened to the money? The profits you supposedly made while colluding with Cheung Qidd?" He tipped his head and studied me. "The reports I read said the money had never been found."

"You don't know," he said. His eyes moved quickly over me, my face, my body language, my stance. I sensed he was checking the fifty-seven verity tells. "The money was hidden in one of the ice mines."

I'd worked in those mines—except not like he had. I'd used my knowledge to build equipment that eased the physical strain of the mining jobs. Had I never improved our way of working, I might have found the money.

I couldn't say what I would have done with it if I did.

"But Faarstar blew up Plunia," I said.

"Yes. The money wasn't important. It was evidence of my partnership with the council. Faarstar's action eliminated the only insurance I had against the corruption on the inside."

"I think Kentaro is working with him," I said. "I think he's been sabotaging us all along."

My dad tipped his head and studied me inquisitively. He straightened up. "You think this. You don't know this. Why does it concern you?"

"I found something in his file. Something that connects him to Mattix Dusk. He may be working for Faarstar."

My dad pressed his lips together, and then put his hand on my forearm and squeezed. "Kentaro has no loyalty to Faarstar. He would have died if not for the kindness of a stranger who saw to his recovery."

"Who?"

"The stranger's identity is best kept secret for all parties involved. Faarstar does not need fuel to add to his fire. When we turn him over to the council, there will be no need to protect anyone anymore."

"We're not at Saturn yet." I pointed to the ceiling. "This attack is Faarstar's army. They're using an attractor beam to lock onto the ship and shake us."

My dad's expression changed, his eyes squinting and his mouth turning down. "They learned about attractor beams from me."

"I know." I considered how indefinable the line was between good intentions and evil ones. "The Moon Unit 7 series wasn't cleared for use, and I don't know how much longer we can take this."

My dad pointed to the doors of Ion-54. "Stay with the Gremlons. I'm going to engineering to pilot the ship manually."

We went in separate directions. Inside Ion-54, the multifaceted silver orb was worse for wear. I wondered what the Gremlons had done to make several of the small silver squares come loose. A Gremlon was swinging from it and rays of reflected light from the squares still attached bounced over the walls and the floor and the faces of the others below him. Empty packages of freeze-dried ice cream were scattered on the colorful dance floor.

My arrival sent most of the pink aliens to huddle in a tight cluster, watching me with wide eyes and guilty expressions. I located Pika at the same time she spotted me. She separated from the group and approached with her hands out. Twice she pulled her hands in toward her body as if fighting the urge to grab Cat from me.

I bent down and spoke directly to Cat. "Activate defensive program. Protect Pika and her friends at all costs."

Cat meowed.

"Pika, listen carefully. There's a bad man on this ship. He doesn't like me, and he doesn't like the giant. I don't know where the bad man is hiding, and I don't know what he wants, but until we have him in custody, we're all in danger. Do you understand that?"

"Bad bad bad," she repeated. Her eyes became saucers in her face and her lips drew together into a tiny dot.

I held Cat out to her. "Cat will protect you. Okay?"

She nodded again. Her hands, flat with long skinny fingers, came at me. She took Cat and hugged him to her chest.

"Now this is very important," I said. "Keep Cat in

here with you and the other Gremlons. When I leave, I want you to ask him to watch the door."

"Okay okay okay," she said.

But Cat didn't get the chance to protect me or Pika or the room full of Gremlons. Because the doors behind me opened and a double blast from a space gun zapped me between the shoulder blades. I fell, face forward, onto the floor.

40: SPACE DUST

The blast stunned me but didn't knock me out. Before moving, I listened for clues of who had entered Ion-54 and what they planned to do next. The doors shut. Tiny pink fingers poked at me as if checking to see if I was still alive. I brushed them away and the hands, (and Gremlons attached to the hands) jumped back and huddled together.

"Who shot me?" I asked. A sea of faces stared back at me, none of them talking. "Pika? Where's Pika?"

One of the Gremlons pulled away from the group. It was Yoka, the short, plump boy Gremlon who I'd spoken to the other day. He raised his hand and pointed to the Gremlons huddling under the swinging orb.

I rolled over and sat up. "She's hiding from me? From us?"

He blinked his eyes but didn't speak. I looked at the rest of them. "Can anybody tell me where Pika is?"

They crowded together. Nobody said a word.

Something about the scene was horribly wrong. The Gremlons were getting smaller, like melting balls of ice. They were terrified. Whoever or whatever had shot me had been there before. And maybe hadn't left.

I stood up and tucked Neptune's space gun under my arm. "Somebody, please. Tell me what happened."

Very slowly, the Gremlons divided into two groups, exposing what they'd been hiding behind their wall of solidarity. It was a grey alien with a black 2 on one hand. Grey Two, the alien who'd arrived with them by materializer. One arm was wrapped around Pika's skinny neck and the other held a vaporizer aimed directly at me.

Aside from the ring of Gremlons surrounding me and the squares of light bouncing off the large silver orb, the scene gave me déjà vu. It was just like the day Mattix Dusk's space pod landed on Neptune's property and revealed Pika's message encrypted in Cat's still missing data chip. That time the threat to Pika had been learned by a secret transmission. This time the threat was three feet away.

Assessment: Grey Two was armed. Assume deadly force.

Assessment: Someone or something had shot me from behind. Grey Two was not operating alone.

Assessment: Grey Two was using Pika as a distraction. If he wanted her or any of the Gremlons dead, they would be.

Assessment: If I fired Neptune's blaster, I'd have a 90 plus percent chance of hitting Grey Two without hitting Pika. Maybe military would have said those were good enough odds, but I wasn't willing to take the chance.

And I didn't have to. The ship lurched to the left and the Gremlons, Grey Two, and I all went flying. The mirror ball swung wildly and then fell to the ground. It bounced against the floor, sending squares of small silver mirrors onto the floor. The ship tipped again and the whole group of us slid toward one wall, landing in a pileup of silver and pink and purple and grey.

I clawed at the colorful, light-up squares on the floor, trying to get a grip. The surface was too slick. I didn't know where Neptune's gun was. Or Grey Two's vaporizer. I only knew whoever found them first would win and if that were the grey, we'd be looking at the genocide of an alien race. (Plus me.)

The impact resulted in a torn uniform and a gash on my chest. I reached into the neckline of my uniform and remembered Neptune's dog tags. The High Durability Tape had pulled off and left a welt. I held the tags in my palm and closed my eyes and squeezed.

Someone poked me in the side. I opened my eyes. Yoka held his finger up to his mouth and then pointed to where Grey Two was trapped under a crush of Gremlons.

They couldn't hold him forever. I saw the grip of Neptune's gun peeking out from a pile of broken mirror ball pieces. As I swept them aside, I noticed one of the silver squares was not like the other. It was small and flat and black. It was Cat's missing data chip. The Gremlons had had it all along—hidden amongst the reflective squares on the large glitter orb. My hesitation cost me time I didn't have.

"Look out look out look out!" Pika yelled in her high-pitched voice.

I forgot the data chip and turned to see dirty, grimy, smelly Omicron Faarstar towering over the Gremlons. He fired at Grey Two. The alien's body went lifeless almost instantly, looking like dried, shriveled branches on a dead tree. The Gremlons scattered and Faarstar aimed his blaster at me.

The doors swished opened. Faarstar turned. It was Neptune. Faarstar fired. The blaster rays bounced off Neptune's Stealthyester® captain's uniform. Faarstar's angry reaction was enough time for me to connect with the grip on Neptune's gun on the floor. I aimed the nozzle at Faarstar and pulled the trigger.

But the setting on Neptune's gun was jammed. Faarstar turned back to me and aimed. I whacked the side of the gun and fired again, this time covering the baddest space pirate in the universe in the accumulated remains of the disintegrated grey alien henchmen Neptune had sealed in the chamber of his gun.

41: ONE DOOR CLOSES, ANOTHER ONE OPENS

The spray of alien particles caught Faarstar by surprise.

"Shoot him!" I said.

"No," Neptune said. He grabbed Faarstar by the shirtfront. "We need to deliver him to the council. He's the one bargaining chip that will erase what we did." He turned him around and secured him with flex-ties.

Faarstar leered at me. I pushed myself up and approached him. "I underestimated you," he said. "You have more spirit than I'd expect from the daughter of a worthless man like Jack Stryker."

I balled up my fist and punched him. Nothing girly about it.

By the time Doc and Kentaro received the Code Blue to retrieve Faarstar from Ion-54, Grey Two had disintegrated and vacuumed into the chamber of Neptune's gun. The Gremlons had tied the space pirate up so well that the only thing visible from his bindings was his head. Alien grey soot coated his face. Doc raised his eyebrows. I shrugged.

The Gremlons crowded around the body and kicked at him with their soft, pink feet. I knew I was witnessing a shift in an otherwise peaceful culture that had now seen evil up close. It was the end of one era, but the beginning of another. The Gremlons would soon learn ways to defend themselves instead of playing dead and becoming easy targets. Evolutionary behavior in motion.

Once Doc moved Faarstar to Medi-Bay for containment (he *was* covered in unanalyzed space cooties), our most significant problem was solved.

I didn't know how to explain to the FC that a robot had killed a space courier. Would they care like I had? Or would they dismiss Mattix's death as a risk of his job? And if Neptune and my dad were right about corruption inside the council, would my report accomplish anything or just alert them that we knew more than we should?

When Rebel Rune and his buddies first arrived, Faarstar's ships scattered like space roaches. Our radar showed no indications that they were nearby, but that's the problem with evil forces. Even when we turned on the exterior buffers of static electricity to counter a new attractor beam, we would be vulnerable until we landed. The AstroNovas escorted us to Saturn, while my dad piloted the ship under Neptune's orders to a smooth landing.

I stood by a window toward the back of the ship and stared outside at Saturn's surface. The once-unlivable planet was now covered with a series of clear bubbles that were supplied with a fresh mix of nitrogen and oxygen with a couple of other junk gasses, the closest mix you could find to resemble the atmosphere on planet Earth.

Even though there were still space pirates operating in the galaxy, for the first time in a long time, I felt satisfied. Maybe it was knowing Jack Stryker was the only relative I had left in life. Maybe it was living through this experience with him, working together as knowledgeable adults instead of a father who brings home busted radios for his daughter to take apart and rebuild. I'd seen flashes of pride in his face and I'd be lying if I said it hadn't affected me.

From my viewpoint, I saw a small group of officials waiting on the landing pad to greet us. Rune had confirmed that he contacted both Federation Council and Moon Unit Corporation before deploying his squadron to help us. The convex window distorted the people, but amongst the group, one stood out. One purple man, about my age, smooth, shaved head and bright green eyes. He stood proudly, head and shoulders above the others.

It was Vaan Marshall, fellow Plunian, my first love, and the single member of the council to recuse himself from the vote to cast my dad into prison for life. Did Vaan know there were questions about Federation Council's loyalties? Was he part of the problem or part of the solution? Was this the idea of a Federation Council joke? If so, they were meaner than I thought.

Vaan wore the rich blue ceremonial robes of the council. His hands were clasped in front of him, hidden beneath long, bell sleeves trimmed in silver. He watched the landing stairs with no visible emotion. The council had done a good job teaching him to project neutrality.

Kentaro surprised me by joining me at the small window.

"I didn't think we were going to make it," he said. "It's because of you that we did."

"I don't deserve any credit. I suspected everybody on this ship at one time or another. You're supposed to trust your crew, not watch them secretly or try to catch them slipping up."

"You suspected me the most, didn't you?"

I'd been right about the clues that pointed to medic but missed one big thing. T-Fal. Faarstar had rewired the robot to kill. Mattix had been his first victim. What none of us knew was that Kentaro had programmed T-Fal with a kill switch of his own. When certain words were strung together in his command codes, he initiated a self-destruct program. He'd enlisted the help of his new friend Cat to run that program, which explained what I'd discovered in the hallway.

I turned away from the window and studied the medic. "Pika was with Mattix when he was killed. She used my robot cat to make a video. T-Fal was in the frame.

He's your robot so it wasn't a stretch for me to think you might have been there too." I paused for a brief moment. "And when I accessed your historical documents, I read what really happened the night you were injured."

Kentaro smiled a sad smile. "I've had five different doctors look at my medical chart. I have the best prosthetic money can buy, but the damage done by that alien virus will keep me in pain for the rest of my life."

"I heard your life was saved by a stranger."

"I was saved by a Plunian who packed my injury in dry ice before help arrived. I may have chronic pain, but I'm alive."

"A Plunian. Who happened to be traveling with dry ice." Neither one of us said the name Jack Stryker. Neither of us had to. My dad had been working deep in the pirate organization and he'd risked it all to save an injured medic that no one else bothered to help.

"You hired Mattix to bring you medication, didn't you?"

He nodded. "He was a good guy who got mixed up with the wrong people. He would have liked knowing you fought to bring his killer to justice."

"It's a shame T-Fal's database melted down. What he recorded on this trek alone would be worth something in the fight against the pirate armies."

Kentaro smiled. "When I programmed T-Fal, I built in a failsafe for his databanks. That information was protected behind a heat shield. I plan to turn it over to the council."

"You're a trained medic," I said. "How do you know so much about computer programming?"

"The same way the daughter of a dry ice miner does. I taught myself what I had to learn to survive."

The Moon Unit Mini 7.2 hatch opened, and the landing gear slowly unfolded. The first person off the ship was Doc. He rolled a hermetically sealed coffin with a portable air tank. Faarstar. Two space police like the ones who had arrested my dad came forward and took the rolling cart from Doc and removed it from sight.

Next came my dad. He descended the stairs and approached the group. I forced myself to watch. When I thought back to this moment, I wanted to have the image of one Plunian shackling another frozen into my memory. There were so few of us left in the galaxy that it would forever remind me how far I'd come from the days when Vaan and I spent our nights together, talking about the future we'd someday share.

I braced myself for a scene that didn't take place. Vaan nodded once, a universally recognized peaceful greeting. My dad returned the nod. The three of them turned to look at the ship. I was too far away for either of them to see my face in the window, but I felt like they were looking directly at me.

Ivi's voice came over the ship communication network. "All passengers are to exit the ship first. Crew members—oh!"

A stream of hyper, pink Gremlons ran out of the Moon Unit, down the stairs, and scattered. They bounced and jumped and climbed each other and grinned. Yoka (I think it was Yoka, but it was hard to be sure from this distance) threw his arms around Vaan's robed legs. Vaan looked surprised at first, and then he smiled. He scooped Yoka up and held him with one arm while Yoka ran his palm over Vaan's bald purple head.

Pika exited with Cat hugged tightly to her chest. Recognition in Vaan's eyes was instant. He knew Cat belonged to me. He looked up at the ship, and this time his eyes showed hope. And while Vaan watched the spaceship, my dad watched Vaan.

Interesting.

"Are you coming?" Kentaro asked.

"Not yet."

He nodded. "I'll see you on Saturn."

The medic headed toward his part of the ship and I went to Neptune's quarters. The room was as it had been when we first arrived. Despite his name on the roster as the ship captain, Neptune hadn't taken advantage of the privileges of the position. The bed was made, the thermal blanket folded by the foot of it, and his personal belongings were gone. Only one thing remained: his white captain's jacket, laid out on the table.

I picked up the garment and inhaled the scent of him. He wasn't even present in the room and I started to glow. I folded the sleeves in one at a time and then doubled the jacket over itself and tucked it into my backpack. When I gave my feedback to the uniform company, I'd tell them it had been destroyed in flight.

"Stryker." I turned slowly. Neptune was dressed in his black military-issue cargo gear. The picture of intimidation to anyone other than me. "It's time to leave."

I nodded. Swirling emotions filled me. I slung my backpack over one shoulder, grabbed my suitcase of oxygen canisters, and left.

There was so much I wanted to say. I wanted a debriefing in Council Chambers and a private session to discuss recommendations for future trips. I wanted to run to the uniform ward and make sure it was to standard so Moon Unit Corporation knew I took my role seriously. I wanted to carve my initials on the wall of Ion-54, "Stryker was here," and leave behind a permanent mark of my presence.

I didn't.

As I climbed down the staircase of the Moon Unit Mini 7.2, I felt the rising tension of seeing Vaan again. So many truths had been exposed since the last time I'd seen him when he vowed to initiate proceedings against Neptune. And here I was, the second to last person to get off the ship, with Neptune behind me. My loyalties were obvious.

I followed protocol and walked from the base of the stairs to the cluster of ranking officers waiting to greet us.

Vaan set Yoka down and squared his shoulders. "This

isn't you, Sylvia," he whispered. "I'll do what I can to isolate you from council punishment." He turned to the military police on either side of him. "Escort Sylvia Stryker to debriefing with her father," he said, "and place Neptune under arrest."

"What?" I watched, helpless, as the men bound Neptune's hands in front of him and shackled his ankles

"You are being placed under arrest for impersonating a captain and hijacking a Moon Unit," Vaan said.

I grabbed Vaan's arm and turned him toward me. "Neptune is a hero. He delivered Omicron Faarstar. You should be giving him the medal of commendation, not arresting him."

Vaan stared at me for a moment. His wideset, green eyes left my face for a moment, seeming to note the dog tags around my neck. He turned back to Neptune. "You will serve time in a Federation Council prison of undisclosed location until a trial date is set. Do you understand these charges?"

"Yes," Neptune said.

The MPs moved to either side of Neptune and prodded him to walk. I didn't know whether the crew was still on the landing pad or if they'd been ushered out of view of the man they knew only as captain being arrested for bogus crimes. Official or not, Neptune *had* been our captain. Without his actions and critical thinking, we'd all be dead.

I pushed Vaan out of the way and planted myself in

front of the police.

"Move, lieutenant," one said.

I ignored him. "You knew this was going to happen, didn't you?" I said to Neptune. "You knew from the start. Federation Council isn't here because Doc called them, they're here because *you* called them. You asked Federation Council for their help when we stole the ship and they ignored us. You're going along with this because you want to know why."

"We had a good run, Stryker, but all good things must end."

"My education isn't finished."

His eyes bore into mine. Where in the past I'd thought the blackness of his eyes hid the memories of what he'd seen, today, they showed trust, pride, and confidence. They showed hope. He glanced down at the handcuffs on his wrists and back up at me, so quickly I doubted anyone else noticed. "There is one last thing you could help me with," he said. "Consider it your final exam."

I stood on the toes of my gravity boots and got as close to his ear as I could. "You're worth more to me alive than dead," I whispered. "Let's call this a teachable moment." I dropped down from my tip-toes and raised my eyebrows, waiting for his response.

"It's a deal," he said. And right before the MPs took him away, I swear he winked.

ACKNOWLEDGMENTS

Thank you for following me into space! Time spent in Sylvia's world is a special mental vacation, and I hope you enjoyed your stay.

Thank you to Eva Hartmann from Your Fiction Editor. I love that you take the story seriously even if it's infused with humor. Your editorial comments help put Sylvia and company's adventures on solid footing (without the need for extra gravity.)

Thank you: Theresa Champion, Captain Flyboy, and Richard Goodman for suggesting elements that led to the naming of Omicron Faarstar. And to Valerie Cassidy, I love your space pirate name so much that I'm already figuring out how to use it in book four.

How many ways can you describe a disco ball that's

not called a disco ball? Thanks to subscribers of the Weekly DiVa, a LOT! Judy, three Karens, Peaches, Ian, Joy, Patricia, Pat, Lynie, Katherine, Clare, Gretchen, Kevin, and Vicky, you'll find versions of your suggestions in these pages. And for every other reader who emailed a suggestion or read one of my books, thank you too. You make what I do possible and I love you all!

ABOUT THE AUTHOR

After two decades working for a top luxury retailer, Diane Vallere traded fashion accessories for accessories to murder. She is a three-time Lefty Award nominee for best humorous mystery and a past president of Sisters in Crime. She started her own detective agency at age ten and has maintained a passion for shoes, clues, and clothes ever since.

Sign up for The Weekly DiVa for girl talk, book talk, and life talk. Every Sunday you'll get an email filled with personal info, insider stories, talk about books in progress, and more! Find out more at www.dianevallere.com.

ALSO BY DIANE VALLERE

Samantha Kidd Style & Error Mysteries
Designer Dirty Laundry
Buyer, Beware
The Brim Reaper
Some Like It Haute
Grand Theft Retro
Pearls Gone Wild
Cement Stilettos
Panty Raid
Union Jacked

Madison Night Mad for Mod Mysteries
"Midnight Ice" Novella
Pillow Stalk
That Touch of Ink
With Vics You Get Eggroll
The Decorator Who Knew Too Much
The Pajama Frame
Lover Come Hack

Material Witness Mysteries
Suede to Rest
Crushed Velvet
Silk Stalkings

Mermaid Cozy Mysteries
Tails from the Deep
Murky Waters
Sleeping with The Fishes

Sylvia Stryker Outer Space Mysteries
Fly Me To The Moon
I'm Your Venus
Saturn Night Fever

Costume Shop Mystery Series

A Disguise to Die For
Masking for Trouble
Dressed to Confess

Non-Fiction
Bonbons For Your Brain

CPSIA information can be obtained
at www.ICGtesting.com
Printed in the USA
LVHW091332160519
618096LV00001B/16/P

9 781939 197528